CALDER COMMUNITY TRUST HOB

I0583069

5 JAN

CANCELLED

SPECIAL MESSAGE TO READERS

THE ULVERSCROFT FOUNDATION
(registered UK charity number 264873)

was established in 1972 to provide funds for research, diagnosis and treatment of eye diseases. Examples of major projects funded by the Ulverscroft Foundation are:-

- The Children's Eye Unit at Moorfields Eye Hospital, London
- The Ulverscroft Children's Eye Unit at Great Ormond Street Hospital for Sick Children
- Funding research into eye diseases and treatment at the Department of Ophthalmology, University of Leicester
- The Ulverscroft Vision Research Group, Institute of Child Health
- Twin operating theatres at the Western Ophthalmic Hospital, London
- The Chair of Ophthalmology at the Royal Australian College of Ophthalmologists

You can help further the work of the Foundation by making a donation or leaving a legacy. Every contribution is gratefully received. If you would like to help support the Foundation or require further information, please contact:

THE ULVERSCROFT FOUNDATION
The Green, Bradgate Road, Anstey
Leicester LE7 7FU, England
Tel: (0116) 236 4325

website: www.foundation.ulverscroft.com

NOTHING BUT THE BEST

Natalie's boyfriend Philip is a high-powered, successful surgeon. But while she feels safe and secure in his arms, she resents the way he bottles up his feelings; and how can she challenge him about the long hours he works, when he's doing it to save lives? When Philip discovers that he has inherited a dilapidated seaside cottage from his estranged father, and Natalie must undergo a serious operation, both of them are forced to examine their relationship and decide whether it's likely to stand the test of time.

*Books by Margaret Sutherland
in the Linford Romance Library:*

VALENTINE MASQUERADE
SEVEN LITTLE WORDS
SAVING SHELBY SUMMERS

MARGARET SUTHERLAND

◆

NOTHING BUT THE BEST

Complete and Unabridged

LINFORD
Leicester

First published in Great Britain in 2015

First Linford Edition
published 2016

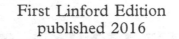
FALKIRK COUNCIL LIBRARIES

Copyright © 2015 by Margaret Sutherland
All rights reserved

A catalogue record for this book is available
from the British Library.

ISBN 978–1–4448–3092–7

Published by
F. A. Thorpe (Publishing)
Anstey, Leicestershire

Set by Words & Graphics Ltd.
Anstey, Leicestershire
Printed and bound in Great Britain by
T. J. International Ltd., Padstow, Cornwall

This book is printed on acid-free paper

In memory of Shadow

1

Here it was: number 10, Beach Road. Philip pulled up, idling the Lexus as he stared at the shabby weatherboard cottage sagging into waist-high weeds. His inheritance from the father he'd never spoken to; never even met. What a joke. The keys were in his pocket. He closed his eyelids and pressed them with his fingertips, as though he needed to block out whatever lay inside.

A wave of nausea brought out a drenching sweat. He thought of himself as cool and collected. Scalpel in hand, he could cope with a severed artery or failing heartbeat; yet this domestic news had thrown him into a state of panic. Why did he even care? His mother's version of his origins had satisfied him until now. His father had walked out on them when Philip was a baby. And now this stranger — a dead stranger — had invaded his peace of mind, claiming parentage. If it was true, why wait till now? No way was he ready to walk into that dump and face the material remnants of that person's life.

He revved the engine and did a U-turn, heading back to the main road of the tiny settlement. The cottage represented more than real estate. It held the secrets of a man who'd left him; of a mother who refused even now to discuss his father. But it would have been better to let sleeping dogs lie. Who cared whose spermatozoon had wiggled its way to the front of the race thirty-six years ago? Philip was a successful surgeon, respected, financially secure, and not bad-looking. Recently he'd hooked up with a beautiful young woman. He had no complaints. Until now.

He was driving as though pursued by the hounds of hell. *Slow down!* he told himself. In this sleepy hollow, people probably drove at walking pace. There was nowhere to go except the narrow shores of the lake. He headed that way

2

now, pulling up when the road ran out next to a small park. A couple of kids played there on the swings. At the end of the white jetty a solitary figure sat fishing. Boats bobbed on the gentle current, reflections of their masts rippling like twisted veins on the restless surface of the pallid water. The atmosphere was a palette of wintery color — cool gray and the washed-out blue of his surgical scrubs. Dark green casuarinas whispered in the winter wind.

Philip lowered the car window and soaked up the soothing sound of wavelets trickling and splashing on the shelly shore. How different this was from the hospital, a location of urgency and crisis. He was used to the glare of operating room lights and the glitter of surgical instruments. Masks guarded the expressions of colleagues. Mechanical sounds counted heartbeats and measured breaths. Life hung literally on the knife edge of his gloved hand. His work was high-performance, with an inbuilt drama he had grown to enjoy.

The most challenging surgery didn't cause him to feel as he did now — as though the fight-or-flight response had taken over his body. He had a mad urge to run away. But from what? A tumbledown wreck willed to him by some unknown fellow from his mother's past?

There was no need for him to bother inspecting the place. He'd noticed a land agent's office in the small shopping center as he drove past; he could simply hire people to clear the furniture and put the cottage up for sale. The building might be worthless, but the land had to be of value, fronting the lake as it did. And there might be paintings stored inside. The lawyer had said Philip's father was quite well-known as an artist. That was just one more bizarre piece of information Philip didn't want to know. Or did he? Along with the mixed bag of anger, sorrow, and rage at his mother's secrecy, there was a searing need to know something of the father he'd never expected to meet.

He stepped out of the car. August

had been a series of sunny, cloudless days — unusual for an Australian winter; but the breeze was cold. A young woman jogged past, pushing a baby in a stroller. The world of the hospital seemed so far away. He was due there for an early-afternoon conference regarding the conjoined twins recently flown in from Papua New Guinea, where they'd been delivered by caesarean section. Their mother was a local woman, married to an Australian aid worker there. Philip was one of the members of the surgical team chosen to carry out the risky procedure of separation. The babies were doing as well as might be expected, given the drastic operation they would soon undergo, but their pre-surgical condition was still critical. Philip had been called in at two a.m. when one little girl's breathing was causing concern. Fortunately the emergency had passed. By then it had been too late to return home to bed, so he'd decided to take the plunge and deal with the cottage while he had a few hours to spare.

So why was he avoiding the issue? If he took the bit between his teeth and stopped procrastinating, he could go to the cottage and do a quick inspection before heading to the hospital. This level of apprehension was a feeling he associated with the past, as a young medical student observing his first operations. But now he was an adult who knew his course, and followed it.

The park was small. Only a few steps were needed before he was at the shore, where frosty-eyed seagulls investigated a rusty barbecue and picnic table on the waterfront. If he gazed directly across to the opposite flank of the lake, he thought he could make out his father's place, its grounds sloping down to the water. Light glinted off the windows of a front room — probably a sun porch. The man might have taken his breakfast coffee there, perhaps sketching the lake with its jetties and moored boats. It was pretty enough. Len McLeod had been his father's name. An unpretentious handle for an artist. So Philip was not

6

just the son of Irene Novak; he was in fact Philip McLeod.

He stood staring at the glinting light across the water until the sun moved enough for the dazzle from the cottage to fade. An intense curiosity fought with his indecision, and he strode back to the car. Unanswered questions about his father consumed him. He would never meet the man face-to-face, but this was the opportunity to put his curiosity to rest.

Philip backed the car up and turned it, then retraced the short route to the cottage for which he now held the keys. Preparing to make a quick inspection, he frowned when he saw a woman waving as she came toward the leaning boundary fence. Thin and ramrod-straight, she wore her silver hair in short curls. As she came closer, a small dog ran out from under the cottage, barking.

'I'm Denise Courtney. Are you looking for Mr. McLeod? I'm sorry, he passed away recently.'

Philip fumbled with the keys. 'I'm

here to have a look at the place. It was left to me.' He wasn't in the mood for a chat, but Denise seemed keen to talk.

'So you're the heir? Do you plan to sell?'

'I really have no idea.' He gave a dismissing nod and started to walk away.

'I'm glad you've come. An unoccupied house attracts all sorts. I've noticed a few people poking around.' Her voice was low and cultured. 'A handyman was making inquiries, too. He left a card for the owner. I think he was interested in buying. He said he was a house painter.'

Philip didn't answer. He had no time for gossip, though the woman was probably trying to be friendly.

'I did see a man trying to break into the back shed.' She indicated the yapping dog. 'Teddy here went and chased him off. Of course the man could have been one of Mr. McLeod's students, though he didn't look the type.'

Philip rattled the keys pointedly. 'I have another appointment soon. Must get on.'

'Am I delaying you? Were you related to Mr. McLeod? He was a lovely man, but shy, you know. Had wins in some of the big art competitions, but you'd know that. Kept to himself, though we became friendly over the years.'

When Philip encountered strangers, it was usually in his capacity as a doctor. He was used to controlled interviews where medical diagnoses and treatments were quickly dealt with and patients sat and listened. Now it seemed his only option was to walk off mid-sentence, but he knew that would be rude.

'I always think a house takes on the vibes of an owner,' Denise continued. 'That cottage used to be so well cared for when I came here. But that was a long time ago; my husband had just passed on, and I was making a fresh start. Mr. McLeod moved in, but he obviously wasn't the domestic type. He just painted.' Her expression was nostalgic. 'I imagine it isn't too clean inside. Sometimes I wouldn't see washing on the line for weeks on end. I would have helped out, done a bit of cleaning when Mr. McLeod had his heart attack, but I didn't like to intrude.'

The dog had approached Philip and was checking out his trouser cuffs. With a despondent air, it waddled to the front porch of the cottage and settled on the step. 'That's Teddy.' Denise's tone was fond. 'Mr. McLeod's dog. He was a dog man. Always had one. Did their portraits sometimes — the only paintings he ever showed me. He probably knew I'm an ignoramus. I wouldn't know how they judge art these days, but I did a little sketching myself. Birds, animals, that sort of thing.'

'So you inherited his dog?'

'Wouldn't say I inherited him. More like he thinks his master's coming home. In the meantime, I feed the poor thing. Teddy won't accept he's gone. I don't know what will happen to him if the place is sold.' She gave an appealing look to Philip, who was rapidly growing tired of neighborliness. 'Perhaps you'll move in yourself and keep Teddy?'

'That's not very likely, I'm afraid. I'm sure the dog can be rehoused somewhere. I really must get on now.'

'Oh dear. He's a Tibetan Spaniel. Bred by the monks, you know, to warn of strangers. Teddy wouldn't settle down. He has hopes, you see.'

'I'm sorry, Mrs. Courtney. We all have things in our life we hope for. Like the rest of us, Teddy will discover disappointment simply has to be accepted. Good day.'

Why on earth had he said that? Even he could hear how pompous he sounded. He was right off kilter today. Without waiting for a further burst of information from Denise, he walked along the path and stepped past the dog, who growled softly. He was at the front door, just about to insert the key in the lock, when the cell phone in his pocket buzzed.

The brief message caused him to cancel his plans; the inspection would have to wait. The other twin was tachycardic now. This pre-surgical period was critical, and the babies needed intensive monitoring. Even so, there was a limit to human intervention. Philip's heart was pumping. If he overlooked speed limits, he could get to the hospital in twenty minutes. He was in the car and gone in a moment.

★　★　★

Pulling his silver-gray Lexus to a stop in the 'Doctors Only' car park, Philip stepped out, jabbing the lock button of the remote and checking his wristwatch simultaneously. He strode toward the back entrance of the hospital and took the lift to the third floor, where he hurried along the corridor to the pediatric ICU. Inside, he donned mask and gown and used the antiseptic hand wash. Through the peephole windows of several rooms, he could see prematurely born babies, wired to tubes and monitors as they lay in plastic humidi-cribs. He walked past them. The sickest babies were situated next to the nurses' station, where they could be monitored even more closely.

Noting his arrival, a nurse hurried to the desk. 'Good morning, Dr. Novak. You must be tired.'

'Why's that?' Philip's raised eyebrows discouraged further inquiries about the state of his health.

'The morning rounds report said you'd been with the twins for several hours during the night.'

'I was called in, yes. How are the babies doing now?'

'The tachycardia has settled and their oxygen stats have come up a little.'

'A little?' Philip frowned as he took the chart from the nurse, scanned the figures and nodded.

'The parents were hoping to talk to you, Doctor. They're coming in soon. Will you be available?'

'I've already had a word with them. The mother doesn't speak good English.' Emotion was too hard to deal with. He needed to stick to facts. Talking to relatives was a job he preferred to avoid.

The deep compassion their worry triggered in him seemed to stick in his throat, making him speechless. He wondered how other doctors simply regarded it as part of the job.

But the nurse wasn't letting him off the hook. 'She understands, as long as it's not too technical.'

He felt a need to defend himself; to squash her expectations. 'Explaining a surgical procedure requires a little more precision than nursery-rhyme language. But I'll try again.'

If the nurse objected to his sarcasm, she didn't show it. 'I think they're just looking for reassurance, Doctor.' She stood beside him, casting an assessing gaze over the tiny babies in their humidicrib.

Philip's stern face softened as he assessed the sleeping pair. There were no words to convey the ache in his heart as he looked at these tiny scraps of humanity, afflicted so severely by a quirk of nature. Their sealed eyelids closed out the mysterious world into which they had been lifted from their mother's womb. All they had known of human life so far was isolation, medical interventions, pain. Needles had probed and plunged, seeking the elusive veins with their minute lumens. All the natural comforts of newborns had been denied them as they lay isolated from the world. Now they faced the invasion of scalpels and lasers working to tear them apart. Would they sense the loss?

Philip would soon join the team of experts, specialists and surgeons to assist with the babies' successful separation. The hospital authorities and his colleagues were impressed by the ambitious surgical procedure, but Philip wondered. Fused together from their first weeks of conception, the twins' coming independence stirred in him a feeling he did not like. Viewing the bonded pair, he experienced an empty, sorrowful emotion surely belonging to his own past — a sense that he was unwanted and abandoned. Brusquely, he turned away.

'I'll see the parents later. No change to the meds. Page me if there's any concern.' He shed his mask and protective gown. The nurse was eyeing him, apparently approving of his compact, tightly muscled build, his sharply creased suit pants and long-sleeved blue and white striped business shirt. His navy-blue tie was silk; his leather belt and shoes were chosen for understated quality. He nodded abruptly, washed his hands and left the unit, leaving the nurse to return to her duties.

Philip joined the rest of his colleagues in the doctors' lounge. The upcoming separation and progress of the conjoined twins was still the main topic of conversation. The operation would be filmed as a ground-breaking procedure that could benefit future applications. Only fifty percent of conjoined twins survived their delivery. This tiny pair, who were joined at the stomach and liver, were fortunate: they had independent hearts and brains, and the liver separation would not include the biliary tracts. Still, dividing the pair would require all the resources of the city hospital, plus the long-distance assistance of a few overseas consultants. During the eleven-hour surgery, the operating theater would be packed with participants and observers taking medical notes and making videos, as the hours lengthened and scalpels and lasers worked on the tiny forms of the twins.

It might be decades before such a procedure would be called for again at this hospital. As one of the vascular consultants who would play a major role in the surgery, Philip continued to receive accolades and inquiries from his colleagues. He was happy to discuss procedures and possible complications, but his step was reluctant as he returned to the ICU before lunch to meet the babies' parents again. The deep compassion he felt for his patients was so hard to express to their families. He was simply no good with emotional situations. That pattern was firmly entrenched from his childhood, and he'd never worked out how to overcome his stiff bedside manner.

The twins' mother spoke in broken

English that he found hard to understand. She wept and exclaimed, hugging him with a warmth he wanted to back away from. Removing her clutching hand from his arm, he turned to her reserved Australian husband, feeling on more equal terms as he began to outline the medical findings for the conjoined babies. He delivered a summary of omphalopagus development in utero, explaining the fortunate fact that the babies had independent gastrointestinal and genitourinary tracts.

The woman watched anxiously, then flung her arms around Philip, nuzzled his shoulder, and burst into tears. Philip stepped back quickly. He was out of his depth with weeping women. Muttering, 'I must go and check the twins for tachypnea,' he turned to stride away from the two bewildered faces staring back at him.

'Can you save our children?' the man asked. He sounded quietly desperate.

'We'll do our best.' Philip cast a cursory glance over the twins; then, much relieved, he headed to the hospital cafeteria, already reflecting on the afternoon surgery list. A couple of his fellow doctors walked ahead of him, chatting. Philip's stomach still felt knotted. His mother had suffered from untreated bipolar mood swings, and his earliest memories were of her unpredictable outbursts that he could neither understand nor control. No wonder he'd learned to manage his own feelings, though more than one woman in his past had called him cold and unemotional.

Outside the cafeteria, he checked the blackboard menu. Often he skipped lunch, preferring to enjoy the evening meal at home, but his partner Natalie was away at a conference in Sydney and hadn't advised him when she would be returning. She'd been annoyed with him for cancelling his agreement to go with her. He felt a stab of resentment. Surely she could see his presence at the hospital was more important than gallivanting off to Sydney? Her bad mood and subsequent silence made him suspect he shouldn't expect a cozy home-cooked meal with her that evening, even if she did come home. He hoped her mood would have improved by then. Sharing his living space had been a big concession for a man used to solitude. Natalie's beauty was entrancing, and she was an enthusiastic bed partner, but she was only in her mid-twenties. Her initial independence had made Philip hope she would understand the demands of his profession, but time was proving him wrong. She wanted company and attention.

But he didn't want to think about that now. He took a tray, cutlery, and a paper napkin, and joined the queue. When he got to the front he ordered baked fish with vegetables and chips, then paid at the till, noting absently that the cashier had an obvious goiter and looked thyrotoxic. He carried his tray to an unoccupied table, well away from the group of nurses gathered to celebrate a birthday. Their singing died away, replaced by giggles and high-pitched laughter.

Philip ate methodically, not noticing the taste of the food. There was to be another important consultation with the anesthetists who would be involved with the separation surgery. This kind of high-risk intervention put ongoing pressure on the whole team. The babies would need continual monitoring of the portal blood supply and biliary ducts, and any unpredictable vascular findings that might develop would have to be dealt with. Such radical surgery would challenge an adult body. This pair of infants weighed less than two kilograms. Their fragility could result in a crisis at any moment.

Suddenly Philip felt exhausted. Leaning his head back, he closed his eyes. The broken night, the stress over discovering the information about his father, and the risky surgery ahead had drained his normal sense of detachment and control. Sleep would help, but he wouldn't be off duty for several hours. Fortunately his afternoon load was light — a straightforward case of varicose veins, a couple of clinic interviews, and a check of next week's theater schedules.

A nurse walked toward him, smiling. He wasn't in the mood for company, yet was disappointed when she only asked to borrow a chair and moved on, her full buttocks swelling against the thin material of her uniform trousers. An image of Natalie, slim and sexy, floated into his mind. She had a beautiful body, never touched by the afflictions so many humans were susceptible to. Natalie decorated life. But he shouldn't expect her to understand his calling.

At first he'd found her radiant vitality entrancing. She had no idea about the sorrow, pain, or terminal illness he worked with every day. She transported him to a world of color, harmony and beauty, so lacking from his daily experience at the hospital. A few nights ago she'd sat on his knee, trying to manipulate him to go with her to Sydney. 'You know I'm irresistible!' she'd purred.

'Yes! You are.' He'd pulled her hard

against him ... but had remained adamant. He had to be on call for the twins. Sydney was simply too far for him to go with her. Natalie had tossed her dark hair and stormed off to pack. She'd left without saying goodbye and he hadn't heard from her since.

Common sense should have told him she wasn't a suitable partner — or he wasn't. He could have avoided their problems if he'd chosen a woman in her thirties, preferably a nurse, who would have understood the priorities of sick patients. This romantic rift couldn't be happening at a worse time.

Letting his thoughts drift, he scanned the large glass doors that in summer opened onto a small courtyard. An artist had designed an oasis in that outdoor space. Palms, ferns and climbing vines surrounded a trickling water feature. The modern sculpture was at first glance just a hunk of black stone, but contemplation transformed it into a human figure, conveying tenderness as it offered a protective embrace to a smaller being. The impression of gentle nurture brought tears to Philip's eyes and a sense of disbelief. Why on earth did he want to cry? He was a surgeon! He'd had the same reaction in ICU, gazing at those vulnerable mites in their cot. Perhaps he needed to prescribe himself a mild mood enhancer.

Packing his dishes neatly on his tray, he pushed back his chair and left the cafeteria. Preparing to head to his afternoon appointments, he stood, irresolute, then turned. He should catch up with paperwork and review that journal article on peripheral vascular disease, but his legs were steering him in the opposite direction, toward the lifts. A plump, pretty nurse emerged from a side ward, scattering papers as she almost bumped into him. 'Doctor! Sorry!' Accepting her flustered apology, he offered a smile and stooped to help gather the fallen pages. They looked like children's brightly crayoned pictures. He recognized the nurse now — Jane someone; she'd worked with him on a couple of recent cases. Last year she'd married one of the ambulance drivers and he'd contributed to the staff gift voucher.

'We had a coloring competition on the ward,' she said. 'I'm going to make a display of these in the corridor. The walls have a sterile look, don't you think?'

Philip eyed the bland cream expanses of paint that stretched away into the distance. Perhaps she was right. He wasn't observant in that way. His mind was usually occupied with medical issues. Meanwhile, patients, staff, and visitors came and went. Wheelchairs and gurneys transported clients to wards. Different uniforms denoted employees' places within the hospital hierarchy. Otherwise, his surroundings were too familiar to register with him.

As he moved on, Jane added encouragement: 'Good luck with the twins, Doctor.' The upcoming surgery was common knowledge. The nurse meant well, but what had luck to do with anything? Yes, at present everyone seemed impressed. The ambitious separation had already hit the headlines. But as a team leader responsible for these babies' fates, he knew just how delicate and risky the procedure would be. Those little mites had come into the world ill-equipped to survive. If they died, the gossip would take on a somber tone.

Philip pressed the lift button, feeling the knot in his stomach. His lunch wasn't sitting easily. Controlling his nausea, he took the lift up to the third floor.

2

As Natalie Norris headed up the freeway to Newcastle in her yellow Volkswagen, she passed a good-looking male driver with a toot and a wave. She didn't need much encouragement to flirt, and she still resented the change of plans that had left her without a partner for the Saturday night conference dinner. She was an interior designer, and had told Philip about her Sydney conference months ago. Not only would there be sessions on the latest trends in city living and architectural design, but she could also catch up with friends, some of whom she hadn't seen since graduation four years ago.

The conference dinner had promised to be a glamorous affair — she'd bought a new dress and shoes and decided she and Philip could hobnob in style. She'd pointed out she never went anywhere like that in Newcastle. It was a down-to-earth provincial city, unlike Sydney, where plenty of people owned yachts and mansions on the waterfront, and wrote five-figure checks for worthy causes. At first, when she'd asked him to accompany her to the conference, he'd agreed. There were a couple of medical research projects he said he'd like to catch up on at Prince Alfred Hospital while Natalie attended her conference. Afterwards they could take an extra couple of days off to enjoy a holiday, their first real break together since they'd met. Natalie had suggested an evening at the Opera House and a night of luxury at a Blue Mountains resort, to celebrate Christmas in July. But then the twins had arrived, and Philip had cancelled at the last minute. Natalie couldn't even complain. The conjoined twins had been on the news all week as the preparations for their surgery escalated.

'You can see why I have to be on call.' Philip had been matter-of-fact about the change of plan. 'This period is critical. Any number of things could go wrong. I have to be here, Natalie.'

She'd felt bitterly disappointed. It wasn't just a case of the sick babies. Philip was always messing her around, changing plans, cancelling dinners, or simply saying he was dead tired after a long day operating. Natalie watched late shows and old movies on her own, wondering why her social life had been replaced by this hermit-like existence.

On the morning she left, she hadn't bothered to say goodbye. Nor had she telephoned Philip once, deliberately switching off her cell phone and filling every hour of the weekend with activity. Several overseas speakers had shared the latest trends in design. There were workshops, social get-togethers, and of course the conference dinner. Unpacking her glittering red sheath dress and matching heels, she'd refused to give in to self-pity. If she had to walk into the dinner alone, she'd do it with her head held high and looking her best. She'd wound her long dark hair into a knot at the nape of her neck, trailing shorter front curls to frame her oval face. Dramatic makeup suited the occasion and she'd gone to town with mascara, liner and shadow, enhancing her dark brown eyes. By the time she'd applied foundation and a hint of blush, she surveyed herself with approval in the hotel room mirror. She was ready.

Seated between two men, she made a point of establishing that she was open to invitations. One man had suggested they go to a club afterwards. The other had invited her on a day cruise to Parramatta after the conference. She'd refused both offers. Her vanity was satisfied, but she was only playing. Philip wasn't there, and his absence had spoiled the weekend. Excusing herself, she'd moved to another table to catch up with Danielle, an old friend from design college.

'You look stunning!' were Danni's first words, but they only reinforced Natalie's self-doubt. This was a work conference.

She would have preferred to impress with some outstanding design vision rather than turning up at the ball like a provincial Cinderella, minus prince.

'I saw you making eyes at that hunk you were dancing with,' Danni went on. 'What happened to that doctor you hooked up with? Get tired of the strong, silent type?'

'We're still together,' Natalie explained. 'Philip had to work this weekend.'

'How long's it been? Three months?'

'Yeah. About my average.' Natalie grinned.

'You're such a flirt!'

Natalie laughed. 'Can't help myself. I was born that way.'

'You wait. You'll fall in love one day,' Danni said with a grin.

'Maybe. If I ever meet the right guy.'

'Nothing but the best for you, eh?'

Natalie snorted. 'Dream on. There's no such man. I'd rather be rich!'

'How's that side of life for you? Much happening in Newcastle?'

'Fairly quiet. The makeover of Philip's

apartment was the last big job I handled. It's been dribs and drabs ever since.'

Danni's face lit up as she shared the successes she'd attracted since opening her online consultancy. 'Since these home improvement shows are rating highly on TV, people are wide open to doing up old houses.'

'I guess Sydney's big enough to support new fashion ideas.'

'Well, yeah. Four million people make a pretty wide net to trawl. You know, Nat, you could join me, if you want to come in on the ground floor.'

'You mean, move to Sydney?'

'We've always worked well as a team.'

Natalie sighed. 'I can't. I already have a job.' What sort of job was it, though? People like Philip were in the minority in Newcastle. Clients were few and far between, and Newcastle wasn't a hub of fashion. Rather than study the latest trends in home design, working people were more inclined to splash their money on poker machines and meat raffles at the club. She shook her head, wondering if she was doing the right thing by refusing her friend's offer.

★ ★ ★

After saying goodbye, Natalie was soon on the home stretch, her egg-yolk-yellow Volkswagen darting in and out of the stream of sensible white and silver vehicles heading north. She'd dropped her cell phone on the passenger seat, but left it switched on so she could hear if Philip decided to phone her. Not that she would take the call. She'd made a point of being unavailable during the conference and afterwards. Philip needed to know she didn't like their plans being cancelled at the last minute. He might be a hot-shot surgeon, but she wasn't some junior nurse he could order around.

The turnoff from the freeway was coming up. As she prepared to veer into the exit lane, it happened. Her foot moved instinctively toward the brake. The oddest sensation took over her body. Her vision blurred and just for a moment her mind went blank. Where was she? Who was she? The car continued to roll along in the traffic stream, apparently driving itself. She did not know how to steer or stop. She blinked urgently and shook her head, feeling her mind clear. A warning toot blared and a black SUV careered past her, only inches from her side mirror. It was a miracle he hadn't sideswiped her.

Shakily, she edged into the exit lane and took the Newcastle off-ramp. Green paddocks soon gave way to outlying suburbs that became more densely populated as she approached the city. Shopping malls, crowded during the day, were now emptying, steady lines of cars forming an unbroken line in the fading light of a winter's late afternoon. That strange episode had alarmed her.

As a large fast-food billboard caught her attention, she swerved into the drive-through lane. She must need something to eat. Philip wouldn't know she was on her way home yet and there wouldn't be much in their fridge. His fridge, she meant. Nothing really felt like hers, though she'd been living with him since Easter. True, she'd planned the décor and selected the furnishings, but that had been a business deal; Philip had employed her to furnish his high-rise apartment. She'd strolled round the empty, colorless space, assessing the attractive doctor's taste and ruling out the styles of industrial, retro, and modern vintage. Certainly not the place for wild wallpapers or in-your-face statements of design. She made a few tentative suggestions, went home and produced a mood board for his inspection. Deciding on a contemporary style, she drew his attention to the monochromatic color palette and minimalist look that employed sharp corners, wide curves, empty walls, and metal accessories.

Philip had been polite and she felt he really didn't care what she decided. At first his manner was formal and a touch shy, drawing out her gregarious side.

But she knew when a man was attracted to her. His gaze held hers and she imagined them in a turmoil of designer sheets. They were lovers before the week was over. They still were. Moving in with Philip had been the start of a new phase in Natalie's casual love life. She wanted him. Only him. But he had another love: his work. Living with a doctor was nothing like she'd imagined. She'd expected a busy social life, the best restaurants, and fund-raising balls. The good life. Instead she'd found solitude and uncompromising dedication — not to her, but to strangers he would never truly know.

Natalie cleaned her greasy fingers on a scented wipe, then neatly stacked her food packaging and put it in the little waste bin she always kept in the car. She squirted a few sprays of air freshener and lowered the window for a few minutes to clear away the smell of cooked food. She was fastidious about her surroundings, just as she was about her dress and makeup.

Dusk was falling as she parked in the

basement garage. Philip's car wasn't in his parking space. Her stomach clenched as she wondered what sort of reception awaited her later, after her deliberate silence. Carrying her weekend bag, she took the lift up to the second level and let herself into the apartment. The cold slate tiles and colorless walls, so soothing in the heat of summer, now created a bleak, unwelcoming atmosphere. The low designer furnishings, carefully chosen for their Hunger Games look, seemed to float lost in space above the expanse of pristine floor. There was nothing in the room that suggested comfort or lazy relaxation. It was the style Philip had agreed to, and it had suited the apartment when February sunlight streamed through the floor-to-ceiling windows. Natalie wondered whether she would still be living with Philip when next summer came.

Dropping her bag, she sat down to pull off her high boots and tights, which felt a size too small after the long drive. She sat down on the oatmeal-colored couch, wishing there were a few plump cushions to lean against. She wriggled her toes through the shaggy pile of the gray and brown striped floor rug, scowling at the only indoor plant — an angular cactus in an oval metal bowl. For a moment, she felt an unaccustomed longing for her chaotic childhood home.

Her mother, a passionate animal conservationist, had been a volunteer worker for a wildlife rescue service. Their home in Brisbane was still a recovery station for injured bats and magpies, wombat babies, wounded penguins, stray kittens, even a New Zealand seabird with a broken wing that had somehow been washed up in Australia. Tucked in knitted pouches, kangaroo joeys dangled from pegs along the kitchen wall. The house had an odd smell, not unpleasant but farinaceous, as though the family lived in a barn. It had been rare for Natalie to see her mother unencumbered by some rescued creature, its bright eyes wary as it peered around a feeding bottle, sucking on a makeshift teat. 'Peel the potatoes, love,' she would request, or: 'Get the washing in for me?' Natalie could hardly resent taking over the domestic chores when her mother was so overworked. There was no Mr. Norris to help.

When Mrs. Norris wasn't nurturing her wildlife, her favorite pastime was fundraising for the organization. She would take Natalie along to help sort through roadside junk on council pick-up days. A broken chair or a child's rusty tricycle could be fixed up and sold for a few dollars at the Sunday markets. As a little girl, Natalie found these excursions fun. She'd even managed to acquire a number of perfectly good toys and games that careless people had thrown away. But as she reached her teens, she was acutely ashamed of her mother, the odd-smelling house, and the ever-growing heap of discards in the back yard awaiting Mrs. Norris's efforts at repair. Natalie no longer invited friends to her home. She became fastidious, used a lot of scented air freshener in her bedroom, and at seventeen she announced she would go to Sydney Design School to study for a diploma in interior design. Her mirror told her she was a beautiful girl, and she intended to specialize in beautiful things. Second-best was not for her.

Yet home, despite its animal population, had been cozy and very lived-in. None of which could she say about Philip's pad. She'd given him what he wanted. Now it reminded her of a surgery. Yes, that was exactly it — a place where magazines lay in aligned piles; where people sat twiddling their thumbs and wondering what diagnosis awaited them behind the doctor's closed door. A place where time dragged and people went home to think about their mortality.

Natalie jumped up off the couch and went to make a cup of coffee. A breakfast plate and cup were stacked neatly in the sink. The shelf of stainless steel canisters had been her choice, like the oversized metallic wall clock. For some reason, everything struck her as ugly. She'd stormed off in a mood, wanting to make her point to Philip; but the truth was that, without him, the weekend had been a flop. After checking out of the Novotel that morning, she'd wandered around The Rocks, maxing out her credit card on novelties she didn't need and wondering what sort of reception awaited her when she arrived home. Some boyfriends were easy to manipulate, but Philip wasn't one of them. When she'd shown him how displeased she was that he was cancelling the weekend, he'd looked at her as though she was a badly behaved teenager.

They'd never had a serious fight. In fact, she couldn't imagine Philip shouting or slamming doors. And she'd known why he had to be on call at the hospital. He'd told her about the babies. He was so reasonable! Perhaps she'd been naïve to dismiss their age and personality differences. What if he asked her to move out? Of course, that option raised a whole lot of questions she couldn't answer. How much would she care, for example? Judging by the way her stomach clenched and tears filled her eyes, quite a lot. Philip was the first man she'd ever respected. She trusted him. He might not be a leather-jacketed muscle-man, but he was strong, clever, and single-minded.

Now she was afraid. She'd thrown a real temper tantrum when he'd pulled out of the weekend trip. And she had deliberately stopped herself from phoning him or sending a text. He might have decided she was too immature for him. At work he would have all those cool, efficient nurses saving lives and making eyes at him.

Perhaps she could cook him dinner. She checked the fridge. Milk, bread, two beef steaks. Broccoli in the freezer. What sort of meal could you whip up with that? Now she heard the apartment door close. He was home. She pushed panicky fingers through her long hair. Why hadn't she freshened up; had a shower at least? Taking a deep breath, she sauntered over to meet him, conveying a confidence she didn't feel.

'So you're home.' There wasn't going to be a scene. He sounded calm, though his manner was withdrawn.

Natalie felt oddly rebuffed. Hadn't her displeasure even registered with him? But there was no point in re-opening the issue if he didn't want to talk about it.

'Did you enjoy the conference?' Philip asked her.

'Yes. It was fine. I was even invited to join a new office in Sydney.' Surely that would get a reaction? Did he never shout or accuse?

'Did you accept?'

'As if I would, without talking to you!' He must think she was totally self-centered. She knew it was time to apologize. 'I shouldn't have laid a guilt trip on you, Philip.'

A short silence filled the space between them. 'I'm going to take a shower, then toss a steak under the grill,' was all he said. 'Have you eaten?'

'Take-out on the way home. But let

me cook for you?'

'It's no bother.' He went up to the bathroom and she heard the shower running. Ten minutes later he walked downstairs, wearing black track pants and a casual red sweater. His fair hair, neatly combed to the side, was darkened by the water. He was a well-built man, not muscle-bound, but fit and compact. His cool green eyes and regular features were rarely disturbed by laughter or anger, so that Natalie found him hard to read as he went to the kitchen. She heard the sigh of the fridge door and the clatter of a grilling pan. Soon she could smell the aroma of cooking meat.

She was out of her depth with this man. None of her usual behaviors seemed to produce the effect that she intended. At first, his title as consultant surgeon had impressed her. But now she was facing the reality of their working lives. Her work paradigm was beauty; his was healing. Philip dealt on a daily basis with disease and death.

Quite a contrast.

He wandered out from the kitchen, carrying a dinner plate and cutlery. Apparently, as far as he was concerned, their disagreement was forgotten. He sat down on one of the uncomfortable modern chairs, balancing the plate on his lap. Methodically, he sliced the meat and began to chew.

Someone had to break the silence. Natalie spoke the first words that came into her mind: 'I think we should change the décor of this room. It's rather sterile.'

'What?' He sounded puzzled. 'I thought this was the way you planned it.'

'Well — yes. I did.' He had paid her to design this interior, but she wanted to live in a home, not a concept. 'You don't feel this room's drab?'

'No. I think it's restful. But if you want to change it, go ahead. What were you thinking?'

'Maybe some cushions. I saw a new line at Clovelly Boutique in Randwick. Really gorgeous. Shot silk, flaming purples, turquoise and gold.'

'Not gaudy? I expect you're the expert.' His tone was weary. 'Order them then, Natalie. I'm sorry, but I'm bushed tonight.' When he turned on the TV she gathered that was all he intended to say.

'I might as well go up and change too.'

He nodded. 'I want to catch the news. There was a press conference about the twins. I wonder how the media will report the surgery.'

'You're on TV? Why didn't you say?'

He shrugged. 'Just a brief interview. I wasn't in favor of it, but you know how the hospital likes publicity.'

Wasn't he going to say anything about Friday night, or the way she'd slammed out of the apartment without saying goodbye? Disconcerted, Natalie went to shower. Instead of throwing on old clothes, she deliberately chose a see-through nightdress. She tied the sash of her cream satin wrap, used a glossy lipstick, and sprayed perfume liberally. Words weren't working. Maybe sex would.

Downstairs, she saw Philip had turned off the sound on the TV. She watched for a moment, silenced, feeling like one of those actors mouthing their lines. She posed, holding Philip's gaze as it lingered on her supple body. Oh, he was a hard man to talk to! 'Did they show the interview?' she asked.

'Just a few comments.'

'You don't approve?'

'The days of the freak show circus should be gone.' He sounded disgusted.

'Aren't you being harsh? Most people just want to know the babies will survive. You should be proud you're involved.'

'That's rich, when you expected me to take off and leave them.'

So he was feeling resentful after all! 'Philip! You didn't tell me there was any risk. Why are you so touchy?' Her voice softened. 'Has something gone wrong at work?'

'Not at work. Everything's fine.'

It dawned on Natalie that he wasn't punishing her with his withdrawn manner; he was genuinely upset. She wondered why, and asked him.

His nod was curt. 'I've seen the lawyer and he's given me the deeds and key to the cottage.'

'You mean, your inheritance?' He'd told her how it had come out of the blue. She fell silent, realizing he was certainly not speaking like a bereaved son. Until the lawyer contacted him, he'd never once mentioned his father, and somehow she'd assumed he must have died long ago. 'Surely you're pleased?' She wished such a piece of luck would drop in her lap.

'It's a bit of a shock. The lawyer says he was a well-known painter. My mother always implied he was a passing stranger. She didn't tell me anything.'

He'd spoken brusquely, as though he was delivering a weather report. What story would a small child piece together from those facts? Perhaps his past accounted for his apparent detachment. But tonight Natalie needed to get his mind off the hospital, and his father. 'How about a glass of Merlot and a back rub?' she suggested in a low voice. She fetched the wine and they sat for a few minutes, sipping the smooth blend. Natalie felt a genuine desire to ease his stress. She hoped he knew she was sorry for her fit of temper, which now seemed so small-minded. He was saving lives while she fussed because he hadn't been with her to escort her in her new red dress.

'Shall I turn the TV off?' she offered. The actors were still silently mouthing their lines like puppets.

Philip sighed, relaxing as she stood behind him, massaging the tight muscles of his neck. 'You're a very beautiful woman. I'm sorry I disappointed you again.'

She felt a throb of remorse. Philip was apologizing to her?

He shifted, glancing over his shoulder, his expression concerned. 'Sure you're not too tired for this?'

'I'm not tired. Relax!'

'I forget you're so young.'

Natalie chuckled. 'Don't say that! I

may have behaved like a brat, but I'm actually twenty-six.'

'I know. And I'm thirty-six.'

'Poor old man.' She laughed. 'Time for hot milk and bed?'

'Suddenly I feel wide awake.' He pulled her around, onto his knee, and she nestled against him. 'You're cold,' he murmured. 'Come upstairs and let me warm you up.'

Relief surged through her body. Philip wasn't angry. He wanted her. Reaching up, she released the clip from her hair, allowing it to cascade in a tumble of curls to her shoulders. She went with him up to the bedroom. As he gazed at her body, she felt the familiar surge of elation. If nothing else bypassed his composure, she knew the power of her allure for him. 'Did you miss me?' she whispered.

'Of course I missed you. I don't like this apartment without you.' He tumbled her back against the pillows. 'I hope you're not planning to leave me?'

His words astonished her. If anyone wanted to break up, surely it would be

Philip? She was just a girl who chose cushions and canisters. He was a doctor who could perform complex life-saving procedures. Still she made him wait a little longer, wanting to stoke his desire. 'So, tell me all about your weekend.'

'Do we really have to talk, Natalie?' He sounded grimly amused. This was a delaying game they sometimes played.

'I think we do.' Though even now she was opening her arms to him. 'What will we do tomorrow?'

'All right! I'll take you for a drive. I want to show you the cottage. It needs your decorating eye.'

'A job for me?' As she said the words, the memory of Danni's work offer taunted her. So far, her website hadn't pulled in many customers. She had nothing lined up, and her bank balance was embarrassingly low.

But Philip didn't want to do any more talking, and she surrendered with a giggle of pleasure.

3

Natalie was in the kitchen, preparing breakfast, when she heard Philip bounce down the stairs. His step was light and he was whistling, his energy apparently restored. Whatever else might be happening in their relationship, sex seemed to smooth out their differences.

'Aren't you going to the hospital today?' She was keen to spend the morning with him as he'd suggested, inspecting the cottage. He hadn't seemed grateful or even pleased at his good fortune. Privately, she thought it was marvellous that he'd inherited a property. She had no such prospects. If she wanted the good life, she would have to earn it, and he'd hinted at a job for her.

'I may go in this afternoon,' he said. 'The morning's free. We can do the inspection first.'

'How does your mother feel about

the news?' All Natalie knew about her was that she lived in welfare accommodation and that Philip's relationship with her seemed difficult. The casual remarks he'd dropped about his childhood gave little away, but when he did pay dutiful visits, he was often brusque or withdrawn afterwards, and so far he hadn't suggested introducing Natalie to his mother.

'I haven't told her about the cottage.'

'Shouldn't you visit her?' Surely he must want to know why his father's identity had been kept a secret until now? It seemed such a hurtful thing to do. But she noted his closed expression and said no more. She shouldn't interfere. Her own mother was only a phone call away, but Natalie was slack about keeping in contact.

Philip must have been mulling over her prompt. 'I'm avoiding her. I don't know how she'll react. Dragging up the past might be too much for her.'

Natalie wondered what he meant but he didn't elaborate, smoothing margarine on his toast as though carrying out a delicate operation. His well-kept hands defined his work. It was easy to imagine him as a surgeon. He would make calm, rational decisions. Admirable qualities in an operating theater, but she wished he'd show his feelings. Surely he must be furious that his mother had deceived him about such an important issue?

After breakfast, she left him with his cell phone and went to shower and dress. Her taste in fashion was colorful and trendy. She enjoyed knowing that heads turned when she entered a room. It was the first day of August, with spring only a month away. She was tired of winter gear, and looked forward to hitting the shops for new clothes. Checking through her outfits, she remembered Philip complimenting her on white designer capris that she decided to pair with a figure-hugging crimson sweater and a long green scarf. She styled her dark curly locks to a smooth curtain of shoulder-length hair. Brown eyes sparkling with life gazed back from the mirror as she drew on eyeliner and mascara. She looked good. Ready to face the day, she thrust her feet into high-heeled boots, and grabbed one of her many handbags.

Philip had finished his calls. 'Won't be long,' he called. He usually took a five-minute shower, unlike Natalie, who tended to stand in a dream with hot water sluicing over her body. She went to grab a second cup of coffee while she waited, wondering where he planned to take her. They needed time together, doing everyday things. In some ways they were still strangers. Their first meeting had been business-like, and she knew virtually nothing of his work. As far as she was concerned, hospitals were morbid places. She'd never been seriously ill, and she'd definitely not inherited her mother's nurturing gene.

She smelled Philip's expensive after-shave before she felt him standing behind her, putting his arms around her in a warm hug. He kissed her ear gently. 'Thanks for last night.'

She turned and raised her face for his

kiss. He was certainly in a better mood this morning. He lifted his keys from the hook on the wall. 'You aren't on call today?'

'Only if there's an emergency. The team knows the ropes.'

'And we're going to inspect your cottage?' Houses were a turn-on for Natalie, especially if she had permission to stamp them with a brand-new look. She was flattered he was taking her to view this mysterious clue to his past. The milestones of Natalie's background were facts she took for granted — her mother's generous, chaotic ways, and her father's ashes respectfully stored in the memorial wall at the crematorium. She knew where she came from and who she was. Apparently Philip didn't have those kinds of memories to rely on. Whatever he'd believed about his origins had been wiped out by an unasked-for legacy.

Outside the cold building, the day was thawing. In his gentlemanly way, Philip held the car door open for

Natalie and waited until she'd fastened her seat belt before he backed out into the street. Weak August sunshine announced a beautiful winter's morning. The seasons seemed to be changing, perhaps as a result of global warming. Though spring was a month away, gardens neglected over the winter months were already making their own efforts to acknowledge the change of climate. Lawns were greening again. Magenta and white cups studded magnolia trees, and rosebushes waved a tangle of hips and frost-bitten flowers on their lanky branches.

Philip's preferred taste in music was Vivaldi or Bach. Formal orchestral music played through the sound system as he drove toward the periphery of the city. He was humming, but gradually became silent, and Natalie sensed he was deep in thought. No doubt he was wondering about his father. She scanned the outlying suburbs, thinking they would have been holiday retreats in her childhood. Now, expensive-looking homes were perched to overlook the lake, and private jetties led out to moored boats. The developments gave way to sparsely inhabited land with intermittent stands of bush.

Following the signpost, Philip turned left and traced a winding downhill route. The road twisted right and left, exiting at the bottom, where the sky-blue lake lapped shell-strewn inlets. They drove around its periphery, and Natalie noted that developers had moved in here too. Impressive homes loomed above the road, taking advantage of the striking views. The holiday shacks that would have echoed with children's shouts and laughter were gone.

Philip swung onto a short road that ran down to the water's edge, and Natalie guessed they had arrived. He parked, but made no move to get out of the car. She stayed quiet, knowing she had to follow his lead. His lips were compressed and his arm felt rigid when she reached over and tucked her hand in his. 'I don't know if I can go in,' he said.

She could see beads of sweat on his face. Deep emotions had taken over his calm façade, and he was struggling to find his normal composure. She wondered what was going on. Nothing could be less like a property he would want. But the obvious need for repairs and renovation would hardly upset him like this. The issue must be his father's legacy. What sort of man had lived here, allowing it to fall into such a state of disrepair? Why would a father ignore his son for his entire life, and then leave him a bequest, without the chance to explain or answer his son's questions? Philip's mother was almost as mysterious. Why would a mother lie to her child and prevent him from ever knowing who his father was? What could a father have done to arouse such hatred and bitterness? No wonder Philip looked so bleak.

She squeezed his hand. A dog barked. 'Teddy,' said Philip. 'He goes with the cottage.' That was peculiar too. Who would leave a pet to a stranger who might hate dogs?

'You've been here before?'

'I stopped by while you were in Sydney.'

'And . . . ?' She pushed away a hint of disappointment. The cottage had nothing to do with her. It was Philip's issue.

'Met the neighbor. Chatty soul.'

'So what's the house like inside?'

'I didn't get that far. I was called to the hospital. And I needed time. I'm afraid of what's waiting for me, Nat. I feel as though, once I step through that door, I'll come face to face with ghosts. Who's going to tell me the truth? My father's dead. My mother won't acknowledge he existed.' He raked his fingers through his fair hair in a gesture of confusion. 'I wish I'd never heard of Len McLeod.'

'Come on.' She tugged his hand. 'This talk isn't helping. Let's go take a look.'

As they walked through the leaning front gate, a small dog, its coat a fluffy mix of white, brown and black fur, stood upright and confronted them, barking sternly. 'What a cute dog!' Natalie crouched down, offering her hand to be sniffed.

'According to the neighbor, that's Teddy. He's waiting for my father.'

'That's so sad! Who feeds him?'

'She does. You'll meet her, never fear! She's probably watching as we speak.' He grinned, suddenly boyish. 'She won't miss anything going on here.'

With flaking weatherboards and a rusted roof, the cottage looked derelict. The small front garden was knee-high in weeds and seeding thistles. A few struggling freesias edged a cracked cement path. Otherwise, the lawn was a wilderness of self-sown grasses and broadleaf weeds, edged by overgrown borders. A straggling jacaranda tree shaded the entire garden. As they approached the front steps, the dog backed away, still barking.

'It looks quite old,' Natalie said, gazing at the house. She tried wooing the wary animal, clucking and calling, but she only drew a louder volley of growls.

Philip signalled toward a lattice gate, half off its hinges. 'He might bite. Come round the back; I've got keys.'

In the yard, a clothesline, its lines still studded with colored pegs, had toppled over. Apart from a shed, which looked reasonably secure, everything else was in the last stages of decay and disrepair. Mossy fruit trees thrust up leafless branches as gnarled as arthritic hands. At the rear of the property an ugly cement-block wall closed out the view toward the lake. The old-fashioned outdoor toilet had collapsed, its timbers lying scattered about like a game of pick-up sticks. A prolific vine dangled its prickly green fruit along a paling fence that looked ready to collapse at the press of a fingertip.

Philip had done a quick assessment and was fitting his key in the back door. Natalie followed as he stepped onto a narrow back porch taken up with concrete washtubs and an indoor lavatory. A grimy window shed gray light on a drab pre-retro kitchen. There were empty pots and pans on the stove, and plates and cutlery set out as though in readiness for a meal. Without power connected, there was no way to know if the old-fashioned appliances still functioned. A plain wooden table stood on the black and white checkerboard linoleum. Every cupboard door was painted a different color.

Natalie sniffed. 'Something smells off.' She checked the cupboards and the oven, finding old jam jars and a hardened roll of dog food in the disconnected fridge. It was hard to guess what Philip was feeling. He stood in the doorway, as though not wanting to come any closer to his father's life. She followed him as he walked down the hallway, passing a couple of small, uninviting bedrooms furnished with dated, unmatched beds and tallboys.

Her hopes for picking up a job here were fading. Short of tearing down walls and designing the interior from scratch, there wasn't any potential for her input. Philip must be so disappointed that this was the extent of his father's legacy. The sensible decision would be to demolish the place and sell the land. A developer would snap it up. Regardless of the barely liveable hovel this was, there was no denying its position was superb.

Someone, probably the painter himself, had made amateur changes to the north-facing bedrooms. Badly fitting joinery framed large cut-out windows, and a dividing wall had been knocked down. The resulting space was clearly the artist's studio. There was a long trestle table, one end cluttered with jars, brushes, bottles of various chemicals, and painting accessories. Unfinished canvases leaned around the walls or were propped on sliding racks. Philip opened a built-in cabinet, revealing dozens of tubes of paint. There were easels, an entire drawer full of pastel sticks and another holding palette knives, wads of cotton, and handmade implements whose purpose only an artist would have known.

'I think he loved his work,' Natalie said. 'Can't you feel him working here, standing to catch the light? He probably even slept here.' She indicated an old-fashioned chaise longue, pushed against one wall.

'More fool him.' Philip sounded bitter. 'Breathing lead and chemical fumes day and night.'

'Don't you want to look at these pictures?'

He scowled. 'Haven't you noticed? Nothing's finished.'

Now that she looked more carefully, Natalie saw he was right. Some canvases wore undercoats, scribbled lines, perspective angles. Others were being reworked, new layers of paint covering over drafts that must have been rejected. A lot of the work was abstract, though one canvas showed a blocked-in sketch of a dog. Angled lines divided its body into segments with cryptic abbreviations that might have been shading directions.

'We've seen enough,' said Philip as

his cell phone buzzed. His expression darkened at the caller's message. 'What? No, don't let them in. God knows where their equipment's been. Tell them it's a sterile area. I'll be there in twenty minutes.' He snapped off his phone and signaled Natalie. 'We need to go right now. The media have turned up in ICU, claiming they have a contract to film the twins for a documentary. They probably paid the parents for a scoop.' He paused. 'I haven't got time to run you home. Want to come to the hospital with me?'

'Not really.' She could understand his need to respond to the phone call, but hanging around sick people wasn't her idea of a fun day. 'Why don't you leave me here? I'd like to check out the place again. You did mention the possibility of doing it up.'

'If you like. But you might be stuck here for hours.'

'If I go for a walk, I'll take my phone. Call me when you're on your way back.'

He handed her the keys. 'I'll leave you with these, then.'

'Just go.' She gave him an affectionate push. 'I'll pick up some lunch and explore. I'll be fine.' In fact, she was curious to check out the cottage properly. It seemed a place of secrets — a hideaway for a painter of some renown, despite his hermit lifestyle. And perhaps it held answers to Philip's often puzzling nature.

She stood on the porch, waiting until he U-turned and drove away. Beside her, the dog twitched its curly tail forlornly. Its plight filled Natalie with sympathy. Such loyalty was beyond her experience. Novelty always beckoned to her, and until she'd met Philip, break-ups had been a regular part of her dating life. Sometimes she wondered if the chase was more fun that the actual relationship.

Hearing a friendly call, she guessed the woman walking up the path must be the neighbor Philip had mentioned. She looked to be in her sixties, with alert cornflower-blue eyes and a youthful smile. She introduced herself as

Denise Courtney, explaining she called in every day to feed the dog. Seeing her, the animal ran to its empty food bowl and stood expectantly.

'I hope I'm not intruding? I saw you and the young man arrive. I just wanted to give you this.' She passed over a business card. 'Nice young fellow, about your age. House painter. Looking for work. I said I'd pass on the message.'

'Oh, it's not my property,' Natalie said. 'I don't know if the owner would be interested.'

'Mr. McLeod never bothered with upkeep. He had the artist's inner eye for beauty. His surroundings didn't seem to matter.' With an expansive sweep of her arm she indicated the outlook over the water. 'Of course he had this glorious view to wake up to every day.'

'Was he a teacher?' Natalie knew Philip would be interested in any information about his elusive father.

'Well, he did give lessons. Mainly just lived by himself, except for a young man here or there. I used to see them in the garden, setting up their easels en plein air.'

'So you were friendly with him?'

The well-preserved skin of Denise's translucent complexion assumed a faint blush. 'I was a youngish widow when we met. I wouldn't have minded being more, but he wasn't looking for anything.' She laughed. 'My vanity was offended, that's all.' Surely it was unusual for a stranger to be so frank. Denise had a youthful manner, as though her feelings had forgotten to keep pace with her age. 'We became friends,' she continued. 'I miss him now, knowing he's gone. I liked to think of him mixing his colors, dabbing away at a new painting. There's a kind of companionship, don't you think, even when you aren't with a friend?' She suddenly looked embarrassed. 'I'm rambling. I'm sorry. Sometimes I go for days without meeting anybody.'

'I can imagine.' Natalie glanced at the business card. 'I don't plan to be here for long. Perhaps I could take the dog for a walk before I leave?'

Denise hesitated. 'His name's Teddy. You could try, I suppose.' She sounded doubtful. 'Do him good. His lead's there, on the railing.' But Teddy had other ideas and growled alarmingly when Natalie approached him. 'It's not personal. He's guarding the house. It's all I can do to give him his bowl of biscuits.'

'But he can't sit here forever! What will happen to him?'

'Who knows? I'd adopt him, but he won't have a bar of that. The owner will have to deal with him.' Natalie tried to imagine the dog in Philip's pristine apartment as Denise put down his food. 'I won't take up your time. But if you need anything, you know where I live.' As she turned to leave, Teddy sniffed disdainfully at the bowl and walked away. Denise was clearly providing him with regular meals, as he was in good condition. Ignoring Natalie, he settled again on the step. She decided to stroll to the village on her own. Walking Teddy was a lost cause; he disappeared under the house as soon as she called him.

* * *

The main street turned out to be a haphazard row of run-down shops, a small library, and a gas station. When Natalie asked to buy a sandwich, the server in the fast-food store shrugged his shoulders and pointed to the blackboard menu as though he was conserving energy. She settled for a hot pie and a soft drink, and walked on toward the lake. There wasn't the slightest hint of style or fashion in the poorly dressed shop windows. She shuddered at the thought of wearing any of the cast-off clothing slung on racks outside the charity store. How could anybody live their life here without dying of boredom? Philip's father must have been strange; unless, as Denise had suggested, artists were obsessed with an inner vision and did not care about their actual surroundings.

Reaching the lake, she sat on a bench in the weak August sunshine and began tossing the leftovers of the half-cold pie. Sensing the prospect of food, birds

71

gathered. Ducks and pelicans waddled toward Natalie in silent clusters, keeping to their own colonies. Squawking seagulls, less polite, pushed demandingly to the front lines, while overhead, the noisy twitters of brightly-feathered lorikeets swelled and ebbed. Moored catamarans, cruisers and yachts lay at anchor, rocking on the water. A couple parked their SUV on the roadside and opened the boot for their dog. Holding hands, they set off for a walk, their golden retriever pulling like a bloodhound on its lead.

Natalie wished she could relive the intimacy of the previous night. Already Philip was back to being the unavailable doctor, needed by his patients. Who knew how long he would be at the hospital, caught up in the media conflict, while she was alone. She treasured moments when he showed need, but then he took them back as though they'd never been. He was a hard man, and unforgiving. He had rejected the gift of his inheritance even before considering why it had been offered. If he opted to sell up, her hope of securing another job would be gone.

The bleak realization made the walk back to the cottage seem further. Pausing for a rest, Natalie fished out the business card Denise had given her. She could phone the house painter and arrange a meeting. An inquiry wouldn't hurt. Too bad if Philip thought she was presumptuous. She still hoped the cottage could give them a joint purpose, as well as solving her current money problems.

She phoned the number, and a message asked her to leave details on the voice mail. Giving her name and the address of the property, she walked slowly back to the house. Philip still hadn't called. She was out of her depth, looking for the heart of a man who was already married to his work.

Her thoughts jolted back to the present when she saw a motorbike propped outside the cottage gate. Feeling uneasy, she saw someone walk through the side entrance from the back yard. He slouched toward her with an air of ownership, offering no apology that he was trespassing. He smiled, showing stained teeth.

'G'day. Gary Baker's the name. I stayed here as a caretaker while Len was in the hospital. I've got gear stashed in the shed. Lost the key. You got a spare?'

Natalie avoided introducing herself. His familiar attitude made her wary, though he was polite enough. 'I don't have spare keys. It's not my place.'

'No?' He was eyeing the key ring she held in her hand. 'Look, I want my stuff. The place has been locked up for months.' He sidled closer, and his stale smell of greasy food and motor oil repelled her.

'Sorry, I can't help you. It's my boyfriend's house. He'll be here any minute.' If only! Her stomach churned. At least Teddy was on her side. He began barking furiously, interspersing the racket with ferocious growls. Natalie smiled. He must think he was a Rottweiler.

The man's eyes were shifty. 'Can't

hang around. Things to do. You better tell your boyfriend I'll be here tomorrow morning with a mate's truck. I need to open the shed, one way or the other. Best if you can find the key, right?' Pushing past Natalie, he jammed on his helmet, kick-started the bike and roared off so close to the pedestrian walking the other way that he almost ran her down. The woman was standing immobile, obviously shocked by the near miss.

Running across the road, Natalie called out, 'Are you okay?'

'I'm not hurt, no thanks to that hoodlum. We're not used to that type rampaging around our streets. Who was that man?' She eyed Natalie with hostility, apparently thinking he was a friend of hers.

'I've no idea! I'd never met him before. He said he had goods stored in the cottage.'

'I've a mind to ring the police. We don't want his kind around here. I could have been killed.'

'I'm so sorry . . . ' But the woman had no intention of accepting an apology. She stomped away, her posture a model of displeasure. Natalie walked back to the cottage. The day might have started well, but it was rapidly going downhill. She felt deserted. The encounter with the biker had been unpleasant. Philip hadn't phoned, and she had no idea how she could get home.

4

On the porch, Natalie saw that Teddy's bowl had been licked clean. He seemed pleased to see her, wagging his curl of a tail and fixing her with his globular stare. He was an endearing little fellow; a breed she'd never seen, with a squashed-in nose that reminded her of a gorilla's. Natalie pitied him. Without language, he could never understand what had happened to his master. Perhaps she could woo the little creature. Animals had been an important part of her upbringing and she missed owning a pet. She longed to scoop up the animal and take him home, but Philip's Body Corporate laws probably forbade pets, and in any case he would probably go on about diseases.

Where was he? Surely he could have phoned? In a couple of hours it would be getting dark, and the cottage had no electricity connected. She felt stranded. Her cell phone rang just then, but the call was from the house painter whose number she'd dialled earlier. He asked if he could drive round and see her now, and she could see no reason why not. He sounded friendly enough.

She waited for the tradesman on the west-facing side of the porch. The late-afternoon light painted slanted shadows on the weathered floorboards. In the distance, whitecaps ruffled the flat surface of the lake as the breeze cooled and gathered momentum.

Soon she heard the skid of tires on gravel. The driver had parked a workman-like van. The door slammed and a young man came through the gate and walked with a loping stride toward the porch. 'Hi! Josh Reynolds. Natalie Norris? Nice to meet you.'

She noted his light brown hair had a pleasing crinkle, and his gaze was direct. 'Thanks for coming so promptly, Josh.' She could hardly call him Mr. Reynolds. He was several years younger than she was.

He offered a friendly handshake. The touch was brief and well-mannered, yet sensual, as she registered the contact of warm, dry skin. She pulled her hand away.

Josh was surveying the exterior of the house with a measuring gaze. 'My dad's had his eye on this place for months. You the new owner?'

'Oh, no. It belongs to my boyfriend.' She needed to make it clear, perhaps also to herself, that she was in a relationship.

'I'm just here to make a few suggestions. I'm a decorator. I may as well take a quick look around while I'm here.'

'Fine. As long as you understand I can't make any decisions.'

'Boyfriend's word goes, eh?' He spoke lightly, as though amused by the suggestion. 'Lead on, Natalie. Painting and decorating — we'd make a good team!' A grin sketched a few attractive lines on his youthful face. Her frivolous side leapt to life. It was a change to kick back and enjoy a few laughs with someone who didn't take life too seriously.

Josh followed her along the porch, pausing to give Teddy a scratch behind his soft ears. Surprisingly, the dog sat submissively. Perhaps he was conditioned to the scent of a male.

Josh was soon testing sections of rotten wood, even scaling the roof to inspect the iron. Scrambling lightly back to earth, he pointed out lengths of holey guttering strangled by wisteria runners. 'You need more than a coat of paint here.' He squatted on his haunches and indicated a couple of downpipes fallen among the weeds. 'Plumbing, for a start. The water can't get away. And the house needs carpentry. There's a fair bit of dry rot in the window frames. The paint's back to bare boards in places.'

With supple grace he stood up. Several inches taller than she was, his lean body had a look of agility and health. Why was she giving Josh Reynolds brownie points for his good looks? She'd made it clear she was with Philip, yet was eyeing him as though he was a potential mate.

A flush crept through her cheeks and she looked away. 'Do you want to check out the back?' Her voice was formal. She needed to keep this handsome painter at arm's length.

He answered easily. 'Can do. You're not going anywhere?' Clearly he guessed she wasn't living in the house.

'Well . . . my boyfriend's picking me up. But he's late. He's a doctor. He's been delayed.'

The inspection of the interior was just a quick walk-through, but it was enough to give Josh an idea of the general condition. In the painter's studio he stood at the windows, scanning the lake, whose afternoon sparkle was just fading now to the pearly gray of twilight. He checked his wristwatch and Natalie's gaze lingered on his lean, sinewy forearm, tanned from outdoor work.

'It'll be dark in a couple of hours.' He turned from the window, looking at her thoughtfully. 'You know the power's off?'

His concern filled her with a sense of

contrast. Here was a stranger, showing more interest in her than her own partner. Shaky words were suddenly spilling out. 'Philip hasn't called. I did ring the hospital but only got his voice mail.'

'You don't know if he's picking you up?'

'Philip wouldn't just leave me here.' Her throat ached with the effort to swallow her pride. 'I guess doctors get caught up.'

Just then her phone rang. Josh moved to a discreet distance, fingering brushes and implements on the large trestle table while she processed Philip's message, relayed through one of his nurses. There'd been an emergency and he was delayed. He wanted Natalie to call a cab to take her home. This was the familiar scenario. His patient needed him more than she did. How could she mind? What kind of person would expect him to leave a vulnerable patient just to drive her home? But still she was angry. She'd spent all day waiting for Philip. She was trying to help him with the issues raised by his inheritance. So he'd lost his father; so had she, and nobody had shown up to fill that absence with tea and sympathy.

Stuffing the phone back in her pocket, she walked over to Josh. 'Philip's tied up.' Her throat felt tight.

'You're stranded?'

The lump in her throat was blocking her voice. She could only nod.

'Easily fixed. I'll take you home.'

'You?' Her mind filled with awkward questions. Who are you? Why would you offer? What do you want from me?

'I've got nothing else to do.'

'Really?' She blinked back tears. He'd caught her in a weak moment. She felt lost, like a child who'd strayed in a mall and had no idea where she was. 'Thank you.' If she said any more, she would give her emotions away. Stiffly she added, 'I'll pay for the petrol, naturally.'

Josh laughed. 'Okay. Buy me a hamburger tomorrow. My dad will write up a quote for repairs tonight. I'll drop it off in the morning.'

'I'll be here early. Oh, one thing — would you be doing the work?'

He nodded. 'Mostly. My dad and I work as a team. Depends how far you want to go.'

That about summed up her feelings toward Josh. Staring at his lips, she almost reached out to trace them with her finger. As though he read her mind, he smiled, sharing a look of perfect understanding. Was she imagining that Josh Reynolds fancied her too? A shaft of desire rocketed to the pit of her stomach. How could this be happening? She broke the eye contact.

Josh replaced the palette knife on the table. 'This place obviously belonged to an artist. Funny, I wanted to study art, but Dad reckoned it was a dead-end job. Painting houses is a guaranteed income.' He sounded unsure.

'What sort of art appeals to you?'

'That's half the problem. I don't know.'

'Do you sketch? Draw? Abstract or realistic?'

'All that. Call me a dabbler. I prefer large-scale pictures.'

'I'd like to see your ideas sometime.' He was young, and she was drawn to people who saw past utilitarian values. Talking about his dreams, he seemed a bit lost. She remembered feeling the same herself as a teenager. Mrs. Norris hadn't seen any value in her daughter's choice of career. 'Tarting up rooms where the pictures are color-matched to the carpet' was how she'd expressed her opinion, while a baby wombat snuffled on the couch and scrawny geese strutted through the back door. Natalie had gone ahead anyway, following her calling, but a lingering tension kept her phone calls occasional and brief. She valued her mother's dedication, but knew the animals' needs had always prevailed above her own. Perhaps that was why she resented Philip's priorities so much. Natalie still came second.

'Shall we go?' Josh walked ahead to the door. 'I've seen enough to arrange a quote for you.'

'You want the job?'

He grinned. 'I reckon. Feel right at home here.' Although he hadn't picked up on her offer to view his artwork, he was evidently delighted by her interest.

They walked past the dog, which was resignedly sprawled on the front porch, nose on paws. 'Is he yours?'

'He belonged to the previous owner. He lives here.'

Josh raised his eyebrows. 'By himself? Bit strange. What's your address?'

She mentioned the suburb, hoping he wouldn't mind that it was a half-hour's drive away. She was secretly anticipating his company with a feeling of pleasure.

They said goodbye to Teddy and walked out to the van. Josh opened the passenger door and Natalie bounced up into the tattered interior, its back seat littered with the paraphernalia of a handyman's trade. What a contrast to Philip's Lexus!

Josh headed from the tiny settlement toward the city. Oncoming vehicles began to shine their headlights as twilight fell.

It was warm in the van, with its radio tuned to some afternoon drive-time patter. Josh was a courteous driver. His body language was relaxed as he negotiated the building traffic stream and gave way to other vehicles. Natalie felt safe in his hands, without a need for small talk. The comfortable silence lulled her into the present, where she seemed hypnotized by the steady humming of the tires and the passing images flashing past her window. The thought of going home to a cold, deserted apartment held no appeal for her as they approached the suburbs, where large homes suggested wealth and prosperity. Philip's residence was still ten minutes away. She wished there was some way to prolong their drive.

'Do you live on this side of the city?' she asked Josh.

He shook his head. 'Mum and Dad live in Cardiff. I'm still living at home. So are my brothers. Mum reckons she'll never get rid of us. She says our lives are too cushy!'

'I'm sorry to take you out of your

way,' she said untruthfully, because she felt young and irresponsible, as though they might follow any impulse offered by the night.

'No problem. I'm enjoying the company.' She heard the note of flirtation in his tone. She shouldn't respond. He was only a kid, maybe twenty-one, and she wasn't a cradle-snatcher.

'What else do you do, besides painting houses?'

'We do repairs — carpentry, plumbing. My dad and I work pretty well together.'

'You're lucky.'

'Lucky?'

'Having a dad.'

Josh gave a light laugh. 'Doesn't everybody have one?'

Natalie didn't answer. He had no idea how it was for people like Philip, deserted as a boy; or for that matter, herself, with only an overworked mother struggling as a single parent.

'My place is on the corner,' was all she said as he swung right into the next street. Could she ask him in for coffee? Not really. Philip's pad wasn't exactly a drop-in kind of place.

Parking the van, Josh came round to the passenger side and offered her a hand down. She noticed the touch of his palm, warm and rough with the calluses of a manual worker.

'I can meet you there in the morning, about eight-thirty. Dad will whack up a quote to go on with. Is that okay? I've got another job to finish tomorrow by midday.'

'Great. There's a guy coming round to pick up his gear. Strange sort of fellow. Quite frankly, I'd welcome a back-up.' She hadn't liked the man with the motorbike at all.

'I'll see you there.'

Their hands were still linked. Confused, Natalie pulled away and said goodbye. The day was ending on a note she hadn't anticipated. She'd started out with one man on her mind, and ended it with two.

Secure glass doors glided open when

she keyed in the pin numbers, and she took the lift up to the second floor. She saw a faint strip of light under the door of Philip's apartment. He must have left a lamp on when they'd headed off after breakfast. But inside, a shadowy figure on the couch moved and her heartbeat raced — until she realized it was Philip.

'When did you get home? I thought you were an intruder.'

'I'm unwinding. It's been a hell of a day. And before you say anything, let me apologize. I'm so sorry I left you by yourself all day.'

'Actually, I got a lift.' She expected him to ask who had brought her home, but when she clicked on the downlights he looked so drawn and worried that she knew it wasn't the time to start another argument. 'Tell me what happened.' She eased off her boots and sat beside him. As she stroked his pale hand with its clean, trimmed nails, she noticed how soft his felt compared to Josh's.

'The media sharks beat me to it. By

the time I arrived, they were claiming they'd already paid the parents for exclusive rights to film the babies' surgery. Admin wouldn't back me up. The publicity's good for the hospital. So the idea is the film crew will be briefed in sterile procedures, and cameras will follow their progress.'

Natalie wondered why he seemed so upset. 'Is it so unusual to film operations?'

'No. The separation procedure should be filmed for research purposes. But it's going to be challenging, Nat. Do you think I want amateurs peering over my shoulder and filming my every move?'

'Of course not.' He sounded so angry; she needed to placate him.

'Anyway, the media aren't making a program for medical purposes. It's a sentimental Sunday night TV tale. And if any viruses or bacteria happen to creep in on the cameraman's shoes, bad luck. Idiots!'

'When does this start?'

'It's already happening. The twins

91

had a small bleed and had to go down to theater. I had these ghouls filming me and expecting a running commentary for their benefit.'

'That must have been stressful.'

'It was a simple procedure, fortunately. I was furious. I saw the CEO and gave him an ultimatum, which was not well-received. I may be looking for another position once these babies are out of the woods.'

'They wouldn't sack you!'

He took her hand into his cupped palm, gently, as though he held a fledgling fallen from its nest. 'I doubt it. But maybe I'm ready for a change. I'm overcommitted. I know that. It didn't matter while I was a single man. But I can't expect you to put up with the way I'm treating you.'

Suddenly tense, she edged her hand free. What did he mean by 'a single man'? Surely he wasn't planning to marry her? Nothing was further from her mind than settling down to domestic life with an overworked surgeon. 'I'm sure they'd

never let you go,' she said firmly. 'You're
far too good a doctor. You're just tired.
Have you eaten anything since this morning?'

'There wasn't time.'

'Stay there. I'll fix something.' She
went to the kitchen in decision-making
mode, just as she'd done hundreds of
times in the past, when her mother was
totally preoccupied with some needy
animal. The fridge was bare and the
pantry wasn't much better. She would
have to stop by the supermarket
tomorrow. She and Philip were living
like teenagers, with no predictable
domestic life. Did she want routine, a
stocked pantry and a tidy life? The
essence of her job might be change
— tearing down and building something new. But at present, chaos ruled.

She found a tin of minestrone soup
and a packet of whole-wheat crackers,
calling to Philip when she'd heated the
thick soup. At the table he ate in an
automatic way, his thoughts obviously
elsewhere. He needed to get his mind

off work. She was determined to get an answer from him about the cottage. Her mind was buzzing with possibilities for renovating. Behind the shabby façade of neglect and overgrowth lay a gem of relaxed beach living, with rooms overlooking private sunny corners or the tranquil waters of the lake. She was eager to assess the house with new eyes.

'I've arranged to meet a painter at the cottage in the morning. Could we drive over after breakfast?'

He just shook his head. 'Can you bear to be tolerant with me while I sort out this mess? I have a duty to care for my patients. And tomorrow I'm going to see my mother. I want to know why she lied to me my whole life.'

'Do you think that will achieve anything?' She spoke gently, convinced that while he was so angry he would only make the situation worse.

'I'm entitled to the truth about my father, for God's sake.'

She decided to drop the subject. Philip's background and his parents' estrangement were really none of her business. 'Then let me take over. Give me a budget figure for renovations and I'll arrange the rest.'

'You?' He sounded surprised.

'Yes, me. It's what I do, Philip. Business is quiet. I don't have much coming up.'

He considered the idea. When he spoke, she heard relief in his tone. 'Of course I'd pay you for your input, like we did here. It would take a weight off my mind. At present, I wish I'd never heard of the place. Would you really take on the job?'

'Why not? It's a challenge.' She laughed at herself. Her job as an interior designer might involve beauty and elegance, but life had other ideas for her. Here she was, back in the kitchen, offering to clean up a messy situation. She reminded herself that Philip needed her support. 'So, give me a figure and I'll run some ideas past you.'

He shrugged. 'Whatever you spend will put value on the place.'

She wished she could be so cavalier with her own finances, which were in dire need of a top-up.

He yawned, then stood up and stretched before bending to press a grateful kiss on her head. The day's stress had replaced his usual soap and citrus aromas with the sharp smell of male sweat, and she wasn't sorry when he proposed a shower and an early night. 'You go on up.' She began clearing away the plates. 'I'm not tired. I might watch a show on TV.'

After catching up on the latest episode of her favorite reality show, Natalie sat alone in the open-plan space, turning over ideas for the cottage. It would be interesting to see what Josh had in mind.

Philip was in bed when she went up. He slept face down, sprawled like a restless child. Careful not to wake him, she changed and slipped in beside him. There was a new vulnerability about him — the masterful surgeon was gone, overwhelmed by an angry, emotional man she didn't know. Surely he knew life wasn't logical and rational? When trouble came, you couldn't allow it the upper hand. Weakness would bring you down. Ever since she'd lost her father as a child, she'd adopted her mother's attitude. Life was a duty to survive, to defy injury and death, to heal. She remembered Josh's confident wave as he fearlessly scrambled up to check the roof of the cottage. Thinking of him made her reject a twinge of guilt. While Philip dealt with his problems, she could expect heavy moods with him. Surely she was entitled to some harmless, light-hearted company?

Wait! What was she thinking? How could she be comparing Philip with Josh? The contrast was just too much. She didn't plan to risk what she had for the sake of a silly flirtation. It might be nice to have the best of both worlds, but life didn't work that way. More than one irritated boyfriend had told her to grow up and stop the teasing act.

Well, she liked admiration! Why not?

It didn't mean anything. But Philip wouldn't agree. He would show her the door. Especially in his present frame of mind. Even in his sleep he seemed unhappy. Now he was tossing and turning, obviously lost in some dream. It sounded more like a nightmare. Was he reading her thoughts? This broken sleep was recent; another symptom to add to the growing list that suggested he was tense. His father's death had shaken him, and the big operation on those babies seemed to preoccupy his thoughts. He was constantly reading journals or pulling up internet sites on that topic. Natalie just hoped she wasn't adding to his problems.

She really ought to be more support-ive. But Philip was thoroughly annoying at present. She reached over and gave his back a shove. He was taking up three quarters of the bed. His grunts and mutters were enough to stop her getting a wink of sleep. If he wanted to make love, she might be more accom-modating . . . but not much chance of that tonight. Banished to the edge of the mattress, she huddled on her side, hugging her knees.

Why did she feel so alone? Beyond the drawn curtains, she could hear cars passing on the road below. Probably people heading to the city for a night out. Philip might enjoy solitude, spending his evenings stuck at home, but she liked going out. She was only twenty-six! As she imagined a night clubbing, drinking, and dancing to a popular band, the image of Josh filled her mind. He'd be an awesome dancer; she could tell from the way he moved with smooth, easy-going confidence. The guy fancied her. You couldn't hide those messages. He'd gone out of his way to bring her home. She was looking forward to seeing him again in the morning.

Natalie, stop it! What are you thinking? She was being ridiculous. Philip was her partner, and she should count herself lucky she hadn't messed that up with her sulks and demands. He could have his pick of numerous women who worked at the hospital. In fact, why had he even asked her to move in with him?

He was stirring. She hoped he would wake up, enough for them to talk. No, he was back in his dream world, unreachable. Out of nowhere she felt the memory of Josh's warm handclasp. A little harmless flirtation couldn't matter, could it?

5

Once again, the cruise control was informing Philip he was over the speed limit. Nerves clenched in his stomach as he braked and eased his car into the row of shabby vehicles parked outside his mother's housing complex. Why did he feel like an overwound spring? Every area that mattered was beyond his control. Natalie was trying to accommodate his work, but he knew he disappointed her. She should be with a younger, more sociable man. Just as in the past, his hopes for a lasting relationship were cracking apart. It was only a matter of time before she moved on. He just didn't know how long that would be.

Meanwhile, the hospital wanted him to turn into a dancing bear, performing his tricks for the media. And how was he supposed to react to the bizarre surfacing of his father, after a lifetime believing the man was worthless? He did believe that, because his mother had said so often enough. Which meant she'd never given Philip the chance to form his own opinion about Len McLeod.

He felt conspicuous sitting there in his Lexus, its silver paintwork glinting in the sun. He'd offered to buy his mother an economical car, but she'd said she was quite happy to catch the bus to go shopping. The green sedan parked beside him was rusty, its bodywork patched with lumps of white bog and its tires bald. This was welfare street, though of a higher standard than the houses Philip and his mother had lived in during his childhood. Philip remembered dingy, depressing rooms in notorious suburbs, where thin walls meant the neighbors frequently shared their shouting matches. Irene and her son's world had been noisy with crashing crockery and slamming doors. How he'd hated it!

By the age of twelve, his course was set in his mind. He was clever. He would become a rich doctor. He would never get angry, stamp around, shout, break things or hit anybody. He would be calm. And if that was not possible, he would at least be silent. He would buy a big house for his mother. But Irene Novak had never expected to own a home of her own. Material comfort seemed to mean nothing to her. She'd smiled fondly at his promises. Stroking back his fair hair, she'd crooned in her foreign accent, 'A big house is not for the likes of me.'

'Why not?'

'It's not what matters to me.' She did not explain what she meant; just shook her head and clamped her lips, sealing in life's hurt. Perhaps she thought it too much to be unloaded on a little boy, but her silence was worse than any words. Her face reflected an unforgiving anger so deep that Philip avoided those questions — especially those to do with his father. He'd decided it was far better not to ask.

At least she was living in decent accommodation now. Council attitudes toward welfare clients must have changed. Some exemplary tenants like his mother, who'd never caused trouble, were re-housed in mainstream suburbs. Poverty and mental and physical handicaps might still live behind this pleasant façade, but Philip looked around with approval at the brick buildings with their wood-chipped gardens. A pair of brightly colored lorikeets swung upside down like trapeze artists, sipping at the grevillea and bottlebrush flowers. Ramps led up to more terraced apartments, where sliding glass doors opened onto small balconies. Up there, his mother might be taking the cover off her budgie's cage and refreshing the spilled seed and water. She hadn't had a bout of clinical depression for over a year and, as long as she kept taking her meds, might be over them for good.

Philip reviewed what he intended to say. He would have to tread carefully. While he had every right to know why she'd kept his father a well-guarded secret, he didn't want to trigger a bout of illness. The gift his father had bequeathed him raised so many questions. The story he'd pieced together from his mother's bitter hints was that she'd been deserted by an irresponsible fellow who ran off at the first mention of a child. But that couldn't be true — his father had traced him. So why hadn't Len McLeod contacted him? It must have been Irene who denied him any contact with his son. That stirred up an eerie feeling, as though he'd been the stakes in a personal battle. Well, it was too late now. The only clue to his origin was an unwanted legacy. His mother must have answers, and he wanted to hear them.

He locked the car and strolled across the open yard. A man in a wheelchair crossed the paved area, offering a cheerful wave. Another resident passed him, chatting loudly to himself. Philip wondered what they did with their days. Probably his own life looked purposeful to an onlooker. So why did he feel his direction slipping away? Problems confronted him as his mind obsessively churned, circling between his job, Natalie, his mother, the cottage . . . He had a crazy impulse to get back in the Lexus and simply drive away from his life. His mother's illness tapped him on the shoulder; a reminder that her genes might be hereditary. He feared her seething moods, yet perhaps she'd once felt as he did now — confused and overwhelmed. He needed answers.

And he knew what he wanted to do with the cottage. Gifting it to his mother would kill two birds with one stone. Whatever she said, he didn't want her dependent on council housing forever. Governments changed and support systems could be reversed with the stroke of a pen. She would resist, of course. Any change was enough to tip her into negativity — even the offer of owning her own home. But wasn't this a perfect solution? In a roundabout way, his father's legacy could be the means to Irene's independence.

Reaching the steps, he took them two at a time and knocked firmly on her door. But the plan that had crystallized so clearly for him seemed to evaporate as soon as his mother opened the door. Wearing a drab brown dressing gown, her hair lank and uncombed, she exuded a whole lifetime's miasma of grief and brooding. The downward brackets that lined her mouth reminded him of hardship and pain. He had an urge to pull her outside and point out the sunshine, trees and flowers. But why bother? She would look at her son as though he was ignorant.

'Hello, Mother,' was all he said.

'I wasn't expecting you, Philip. It's early.'

'I was passing by.'

Without commenting further, Irene moved ahead of him into the small kitchen and filled the electric jug with tap water. She rummaged in the cupboard in a desultory way. 'I'm out of instant coffee. Pension day on Tuesday.'

'Tea will be fine.' He waited while the water boiled and she fetched a carton of milk from the small refrigerator. He felt a kind of verbal paralysis at the idea of asking about his father. Instead he hinted at the subject of the cottage. 'Something surprising has come up.' He needed her to be curious, but she simply dunked the teabag up and down, then transferred it to the second cup. Perhaps her world was mistrustful of surprises. His father's existence was not to be mentioned, not even to be thought about. His mother had eliminated Len McLeod with her silence. Negated him. Wiped him from Philip's entire life, all through his growing years. Except a boy wanted to understand; wanted to hear about his dad. At least nobody could monitor your thoughts. Swallow your words but think what you wanted.

Even now, he found it hard to break the silence. 'My father's dead,' he blurted out. 'I've inherited his property. I want you to have it.'

Had she registered his words? Carefully she set the cup on the wooden gate-leg table and set out plain biscuits on a floral plate. 'It's time we thought about your future,' he hurried on. Anything to fill the silence. He suddenly was six years old, eating bread and meat drippings by the warmth of a mean kerosene heater. 'Your own place. You could arrange the cottage as you like. It overlooks the lake. Secluded. You could have a dog.'

Passively she sipped the tea, and pushed the plate toward him. 'You haven't had a biscuit.'

'I've had breakfast.'

'How are those little babies you were telling me about last week?'

'Doing well. But the surgery will be a challenge.'

'I'm proud of you, Philip. Don't let your tea go cold.'

Philip sighed. 'Why won't you let me help you?' He had to ask, though the answer was more or less the same one she always gave.

'I don't need help,' she told him. 'I'm quite content. You must focus on your work, Philip. It's a privilege to be a healer.'

Any minute now, she would remind him of the sacrifices she'd made to educate him. He couldn't stand this constant harping on the past. He hadn't asked to be born. There was nothing he could do with his burden of guilt. 'Will you at least let me drive you over to see the place? Just take a look! For heaven's sake, Mother, it's a home, just waiting for you to nod your head. It's no use to me.'

'I'm sure you'll think of a deserving cause.'

This was a waste of time. He stood up. 'I can't stay. Will you think about my offer?'

Neatly she packed up the cups and set them in the sink. 'You mustn't worry about me, Philip. I've never cared about the trappings of money. I have what I need. Get to work now. I'm sure they need you there.' Picking up a packet of birdseed, she followed him to the door and stepped out on the balcony. As she uncovered the birdcage, a burst of song followed him down the steps.

* * *

When Natalie arrived at the cottage next morning, the man who'd come to collect his goods was already waiting in a battered old utility vehicle. Should she allow him access? Philip should be dealing with these decisions. It was a relief when Josh pulled up behind her with his dad. Exiting their vehicles, the three hesitated by the gate.

'Did ya bring the shed key?' the stranger asked Natalie.

'No. Don't you have one?' If the stored goods belonged to him, surely he would have access?

'I told ya, I lost it. I need my stuff, so I'll hafta smash a window.'

'No need for that, mate,' Josh chimed in. 'I carry tools.' He indicated a large metal box in the back of his van.

111

'Got a bolt-cutter?'

'Should have.' Josh opened the back of his van and rummaged in the tool-box. Within a few minutes the padlock was released, and the shed door swung open.

Natalie wasn't sure what she'd expected to see. Certainly not the odd collection of pots and pans the fellow began carting back to his ute. He must be into cooking. And gardening. On his second trip, he carried away a pile of seed trays and paraphernalia of tubing, glass and shallow pipe.

'Is that all?' she said. He'd finished stacking his goods in the ute, and came back to give the shed a last look.

'I'm done. Sweet. Won't bother you again.' As he headed back to his ute, Teddy bounded off the porch and raced after him, barking in an aggressive way. 'Oi! Back off!' Teddy was snapping at his ankles. Kicking out hard, the man lifted the dog with the toe of his shoe. Teddy flew a couple of meters and landed, yelping.

Natalie ran to check if he was injured, as the vehicle took off. Josh stood beside her as she carefully felt the dog's ribs for possible injuries. The fall had been hard enough to fracture a bone. Fortunately Teddy seemed to appreciate the attention, and lay quietly, panting and giving occasional licks as Natalie comforted him.

'What a pig!' she exclaimed in disgust. What might he have done to *her* if he'd turned nasty?

Josh squatted down beside her and placed a comforting arm around her shoulders. 'Hey, you're upset. Can I get you anything?'

Mutely she shook her head. The man's callous violence had reminded her of animals her mother had nursed after they'd been abused. 'What a horrible man! I hope he's gone for good.' She realized that Josh's presence had prevented a worse scenario from developing. As it was, he'd cut off the padlock and stood by, making sure that the guy wasn't helping himself to the artist's paintings or similar valuables.

'I doubt he'll be back. He's got his gear.'

'Gear for what, though?'

Josh laughed. 'You didn't twig what he does for a living, did you? He's a dealer. That was hydroponic equipment for growing pot. And I'd say he cooks up ice in those saucepans.' He frowned. 'We should check inside. If he set up a meth lab in the house, you need to decontaminate. Could be an insurance job.'

'Thanks so much for being here. I'm glad I didn't have to deal with that guy on my own.'

He gave her shoulder a squeeze and stood up. Natalie smiled up at him, accepting his offered hand. She was still feeling upset, and it was an effort to turn her mind to business. She'd rather make a cup of coffee, but the power and water supplies were disconnected. Josh probably knew the quickest way to have the services restored, but he hadn't come here to rescue her from trouble.

He wanted a job, and she needed to focus on that and not on his rangy good looks or friendly manner.

'Do you want to talk me through the quotes?' he asked her. 'Dad roughed out an estimate to paint the outside. But he'll need to inspect the inside and talk to you, if you plan to renovate.'

'To be honest, I don't know what Philip wants.' The project felt like a burden now. It had seemed fun at first — a joint project; a chance for them to share. She didn't want the responsibility of spending Philip's money and perhaps running up expenses he hadn't authorized. He was preoccupied and didn't seem to care that he'd inherited a valuable piece of land along with a waterfront dwelling. She should just walk away.

'This place belongs to your boyfriend? How come you're doing all the work?' Josh seemed to be reading her mind.

'He's a doctor.'

'You told me. So . . . '

It seemed disloyal to discuss Philip with a stranger. 'He's a high-powered surgeon. You might have read about his latest case — a pair of twins joined at birth. They're all he can think about.'

'Man! That's amazing. I saw something on telly about them. He's going to fix them?'

'Yes. With the other doctors.' She was proud of Philip, of course. His work was heroic. But at the same time her mind was whispering, *How can you have a relationship with a man who cuts two babies in half?*

'What's wrong?' Josh was inviting her to share her doubts.

She shook her head, wanting to change the direction of her thoughts. 'I'm okay. I just didn't like our visitor, and I hate people who take out their problems on animals.' The plight of the dog was getting to her. For two pins she'd take him home and rehabilitate him, but she couldn't imagine a dog in Philip's apartment. Her mother would no doubt take Teddy, but Brisbane was a thousand kilometers away, and running home with her problems had never been Natalie's way. She sighed. Her pleasure in taking on this project had faded. Philip wasn't interested.

'I'm sorry I've misled you,' she said. 'I think it's best if we just lock up the house and postpone any plans.' She'd wasted Josh's time. But instead of pointing that out, he just smiled. In spite of herself, she noticed again how attractive he looked. It was as though she had a secret camera in her brain, storing impressions of his laid-back manner and easy smile.

'You're just feeling down. How about coming for a drive with me? Maybe pick up a snack? Take the dog for a ride.'

'Don't you have to work?'

'Dad postponed our job. The hospital offered him a cancellation at the assessment clinic today. He's having a knee replacement soon.' He must have noticed her grimace. 'What?'

'Hospitals. I hate them.'

He laughed. 'And you're with a doctor?'

'Not while he's at work! And yes, I would like time to think. Perhaps I should get the services connected. We'll need electricity, whether Philip renovates or simply sells.'

'That's sensible. We could do that now. Grab the dog and let's go.'

'I don't know if he'll come.'

They tried cajoling Teddy, waving his lead. He was obviously tempted by the prospect of a walk, but stood barking, as if to tell them he was on duty and could not leave. Josh bent and scooped him up. 'Come on, little fella.' Submissively, Teddy accepted Josh's order and settled in the back seat of the van.

As though approving of Natalie and Josh's outing, the sun shone in a clear sky, illuminating a picture-perfect image of the little settlement around the lake. Josh drove casually, lowering the windows to admit the gentle breeze. Natalie noticed he was good-mannered, beckoning other drivers into the traffic stream as he headed toward town.

'Why do you keep doing that?' So many people pushed and shoved.

'Pay it forward. What's the hurry?' He flashed her a grin.

'I'm taking you out of your way again.' She felt guilty. Was she simply grateful for Josh's help, or was something else going on between them? Instead of sitting in a dream, replaying old memories and conversations as she often did when Philip was lost in his own thoughts, she was acutely aware of Josh so close to her. Sunlight gilded his tanned arm as he guided the steering wheel with a relaxed grip. She repressed an impulse to reach over and touch him. His hand would be warm, though he only wore a T-shirt and shorts.

'Where are we going now?'

'To pick up application forms for services. Your partner will have to complete them, if he's the owner. Then let's go where the mood takes us, shall we?'

Natalie flashed him a willing smile.

119

Let's face it, she liked men. What was wrong with a little harmless fun? The cottage was opening up possibilities she hadn't expected.

⋆   ⋆   ⋆

Philip's day was going from bad to worse. Confronting his mother had achieved nothing. She'd been happy to see him, of course, until he'd explained the reason for his visit. As soon as he mentioned his father, Irene's mouth had set in the closed expression he knew so well. He was none the wiser about Len McLeod. Had the man deserted them, or had Irene left him? Had he been a wife-beater, a lecher, a man who sponged off others? Philip left his mother with his usual sense of unfinished business.

Matters at the hospital went little better. Just when all the preliminary tests and scans on the babies were finished and approved, the proposed surgery had run into a delay. One of Philip's colleagues

120

had injured his wrist playing squash, and finding a replacement wouldn't happen overnight. Philip was looking through his contact list of specialist surgeons when he was interrupted by a cocky young reporter wanting to discuss a timeline for the proposed documentary. Philip refused to pass on any information. But ten minutes later he was censured by the CEO himself and instructed to co-operate.

'The press has every right to feature such a ground-breaking surgery. The parents agree. The hospital agrees. You may be a fine surgeon, but I'm hearing complaints, Philip. Poor communication can seem like arrogance, you know. What's your problem?'

Rage boiled in Philip's mind. If he said anything, he sensed he wouldn't be able to stop. The truth was that he had no clear or logical reason for his passionate feeling that life was unjust. He tried, but people were unreasonable. Natalie wanted more than he could give. His mother — still the needy, damaged woman she'd always been — refused to help him understand his father's elusive past. He was worried, facing one of the biggest surgical challenges of his career, and his work was being turned into a circus performance.

Sealing his lips in a fair imitation of his mother, he turned on his heel and strode out of the hospital. He found himself headed along the route to the cottage. It was time to put a stop to all these plans being decided by other people on his behalf. He didn't want the tumbledown place. If his father had imagined that an inheritance could make up for a lifetime's absence, he was wrong. So his background was a mystery. So what! His mother was welcome to her secrets. She rejected all his offers to help her live a more comfortable life. Her choice. And the hospital might think he was a puppet, to be directed as the hierarchy thought fit, but they were wrong.

As for Natalie, she seemed to expect some kind of togetherness he couldn't offer. He must have been crazy, expecting a self-centered girl to understand his priorities. For a time, he'd thought Natalie's beauty and charm could cancel all the pain and ugliness he faced at work on a daily basis. He'd used her as a sanctuary. But how unrealistic was that?

A siren brought his attention back to the road and the flashing beacon of a police car. Philip pulled over, showed his license as instructed, and accepted the speeding ticket in determined silence. The cop followed him for a few blocks before heading off along a side road. Another bureaucrat. With an effort he eased off on the accelerator. No point in breaking the law again!

His thoughts resumed their circuitous pattern. What had his father done? There was a wide divergence of misdeeds, from murdering someone to running a red light. Was he really the villain Irene had always implied? It would be a troubling question to carry unanswered for the rest of Philip's life. Surely someone must know the facts?

He parked behind Natalie's yellow VW and walked up the overgrown path to the front door, then knocked. Nobody responded. The back was locked up. Where was Natalie? She'd clearly said she would be at the cottage this morning. Having had enough of frustration, he forced a window.

The shelter where his father had lived and painted echoed with emptiness. An opened envelope lay beside a folded invoice on the kitchen table. So the painter must have met with Natalie. He hadn't wasted any time in preparing his quote. Philip scanned the figures. No surprise that he would have to spend big dollars. Was it even worth doing up the place? His present inclination was to put a bulldozer through the house and dispose of the land.

Walking in his father's footsteps gave him a creepy feeling. Len McLeod was dead. His son would never know the man. Why rake through the past? He'd long ago understood that the twists of the human mind could take bizarre paths. His own childhood had been peculiar, living with a mother whose lifelong condition, he now knew, verged on clinical depression. Mental conditions made him acutely uncomfortable. His brief excursion into psychiatry during his medical training had alarmed and mystified him. With relief, he'd turned to surgery, where the scalpel was clean and quick, and the patient was a sheeted figure, unresponsive and silent.

The woman next door had confirmed that his father had moved to the cottage several decades ago. There might be some evidence of his life here, stored in a drawer or box. Clippings, diaries, letters? As far as Philip could see, the contents of the house stood undisturbed, as they must have been when the painter was alive. In the studio room, brushes were propped in jars as though awaiting a considered choice. A well-used palette wore daubs and lumps of hardened oil paint. Canvases lay about, half-primed or sketched with experimental lines. Works barely begun, they would never receive the painter's vision now. They would probably be valued and, if deemed worthless, would be dumped at the tip. Like his father.

'I hope you're in hell!' Philip shouted the words in frustration, hating this invasion of his peace. He was a thirty-six-year-old adult, carrying on like a bewildered child.

The sound of footsteps summoned him to the back door, looking for Natalie, but it was the neighbor who stood there uncertainly. She'd probably heard him. He had no intention of explaining his outburst. 'Yes?'

She took a step backward. 'Er . . . we met before. I'm Denise Courtney. I'm looking for Teddy.'

'Teddy?' Did she think this was a toy shop?

'The dog. He guards the house.'

He remembered then. 'I haven't seen the dog.'

'Oh my. He never goes away. I wonder if the other people took him?'

'What other people?' Every encounter

he was having today seemed to be with a halfwit. This woman made no sense.

'The young lady who was here, and the painter. And that vagrant. I heard Teddy barking. Then they all went away.'

'I'm sorry, but I can't help you. I don't know anything about it.' With an effort, Philip controlled his urge to shut the door in her face. There weren't many other leads to his father. 'Why not come in and look around? It's possible your dog crept past me and came inside.' He knew quite well, however, that there was no dog in the house.

Looking doubtful, Denise edged past him, gazing around with a nostalgic air. 'Sad to think he's gone. A gentleman. All he wanted was to be left alone to do his pictures.'

Philip cleared his throat. 'I heard he had some, uh, trouble.'

Her vivid blue eyes fixed him with a shrewd gaze. 'You're his heir?'

'That's right.'

'So you'd be one of his students?'

'Good heavens, no. I can't draw to

save myself. No . . . ' He might as well come out with it, if he hoped to pump her for information. 'I'm actually his son.'

Her look was disbelieving. 'Mr. McLeod didn't have a son. No children.'

He took offence at her certainty. As if his father would be sharing the details of his past with a neighbor! 'What makes you say that? I *am* his son. That's why he willed me this cottage.'

'Then you'd know about his trouble.' She issued the words like a quiz, adding an afterthought: 'Things were different, back then.'

Philip capitulated. 'I never knew him, Mrs. Courtney. We had no contact. I have no idea what his life was like. People tell me he painted, he lived alone, he had some sort of trouble . . . but I never knew my father.' Weakness overcame him. To his horror he felt tears spill and run down his face.

Denise's clear gaze was compassionate. 'How sad! So he had a son despite everything.'

'What exactly do you mean by 'everything'? I'm completely in the dark about this.'

The woman spoke softly. 'He wasn't a man who wanted women. That was a crime, back then. I suppose he'd tried to change. They used to say men could change if they wanted to. But I don't believe that. We are the way we are.'

Understanding was dawning now. 'Len McLeod was gay?'

'Funny expression, that. Nothing gay about it. Before they changed the law, if you were caught you went to jail.'

'So recently?'

'Yes. The law was changed in our state in 1982. I remember the year, because it was around the time Len was investigated. He told me he just scraped out of a jail sentence, but he was becoming known as a painter and there were rumors in the papers. No wonder he wanted to live in peace.'

'He actually shared all this with you?' Philip could hardly see his father turning to Denise as a confidante.

'Only on one occasion, yes.' She hesitated, her cheeks coloring faintly. 'There was a reason. I might as well tell you. I was an attractive woman back then. He was a good-looking man. My husband had passed away. When you live in a quiet place like this, you welcome anybody new. I suppose I hoped . . . ' Her blush showed through her fair skin. 'I started bringing over a few things a bachelor would like. Cakes, biscuits, that sort of thing. We chatted about plants. I had a dog then. Mindy. She used to play with Soldier. That was his terrier. Always had a dog, he did. But I think he realized I was open to more. So he very kindly explained . . . Well, you know what I mean. He said he didn't intend to get involved with anybody, male or female.'

'You mean he gave up all personal relationships?'

'Who knows? I certainly back-pedaled! Could be why he never got to know you. Wouldn't want to drag a child into all that business, perhaps.'

Philip was silent. Denise had admitted to hurt pride. At least he could understand why his father had walked away from his relationship with Irene. She must have loved Len, and thought he'd left her for another woman, perhaps. No wonder she was bitter.

His feelings were confused. He imagined the torment of a young man who had drifted into domestic life with a pretty girl, and managed to father a baby, before his real nature became too pressing to hide. In the eyes of the law he was a criminal. How could he explain that to a girl whose innocence was childlike? No wonder he'd walked away.

Footsteps and laughter interrupted his insight. Natalie and a young man whirled through the door. 'Philip!' Natalie seemed delighted to see him. 'What are you doing here? I thought you were at the hospital.' She turned to the tradesman watching this exchange with a smile. 'Josh, meet Philip. He owns the cottage.'

'Hi! So you're the doctor.' Josh offered his hand. 'Natalie needed to collect applications in case you want the power and water reconnected. We took Teddy along for a ride.'

'He wanted to go with you?' Denise was surprised but Josh grinned.

'I'm bigger than he is. He enjoyed himself, once he was on board.'

Natalie agreed. 'We took him down to the beach. He went like a rocket — raced along the sand on his stubby little legs, barking at the birds.'

'I'm very glad to hear that,' Denise said. 'If you plan to be here regularly, you'll be able to help him accept Len's gone.' She'd dropped the pretense of 'Mr. McLeod'. 'I miss him more than I expected.' She turned to Philip. 'Your father had a remarkable gift. I hope you'll discover the positive side of his life.'

'A bit late, don't you think?'

She raised her eyebrows at his bitter tone. 'It's never too late, Philip. May I call you Philip?' Her veined hand with its opal ring rested on his sleeve. 'I'm old enough to be your mother, after all.'

She spoke lightly.

It occurred to him that, if his father had been open to a second woman in his life, he might well have married Denise. She could have been his stepmother. But the idea was preposterous. Being sucked into these emotional cross-currents was the last thing Philip wanted. Had his mother really never guessed that Len was gay? In those days, the issue was far more than personal. Len must have struggled to admit the truth, even to himself.

Natalie seemed unaware of the undertones between Philip and Denise, as she showed him the painting quote. 'It would be great if you could decide while Josh is here,' she said. 'You think I should go ahead with it?' She smiled persuasively. 'I could do a lot with this place, you know. Josh is sure you'd recoup far more than it will cost. As it is . . . ' She turned to Denise. 'Don't you agree? Real estate must be in demand here. Everybody wants a water view.'

'Agents do call on me regularly, telling me they have buyers. But I don't want to sell. Where would I go, except into a retirement home? Not for me — not yet, anyway!'

Philip turned to Josh. 'You want the job? Could you could start straightaway?'

'As soon as we finish up our current work. What about the interior?'

'Have a look through and brief me on what needs doing,' Philip replied. 'Has Natalie told you she's an interior designer? She's the one with the ideas.'

Natalie seemed happy with his decision. 'I certainly am. Especially for that studio. I'll show you now, Josh.' She was evidently keen to become involved. As she led Josh away, chattering about a structural alteration that could change the barn-like dimensions of the room, Philip's heart sank. Natalie should be with a young man, without the problems that presently weighed on his own shoulders. The pair had obviously spent the morning together. Once again she was the carefree young woman he'd been so attracted to, until his own moods had damped her fun-loving nature. A feeling of sadness washed over him. Was it only a matter of time before he lost her?

Denise must have been watching the interchange. 'I can see you care for her. Just make sure she knows it.' He hadn't solicited advice from this stranger, and eyed her coolly, but she just smiled. 'You have that look that reminds me of your father. His 'back off' expression. Len had his boundaries. Do you have any pictures of him?'

'No.'

'I believe I have a few. I had gatherings for milestone birthdays and Christmases. I always invited Len. Would you like me to look through my photos?'

'That won't be necessary. We didn't meet while he was alive. I don't need to see him now.'

Her glance was quizzical. 'I'll say goodbye. Perhaps I'll see you again.'

'I doubt it. I plan to leave Natalie in

charge of the project. She needs something to do.'

'I see. Well, I'll be off. Take care.'

He watched her go. She was a friendly woman. He should have been less abrupt.

He heard a scraping of timber, and Natalie and Josh laughing, as though they were moving furniture. Weary, he sat down at the kitchen table. What was it people expected from him? He certainly wasn't into cozy reminiscences. The sooner he was rid of Len McLeod, the happier he'd be.

6

With the project in full swing, Natalie was motivated to go to the cottage every morning. Once the job was confirmed, Josh and his father had moved swiftly. They had done a thorough inspection of the interior and found termite damage in several supporting beams. Now, deliveries of timber and hardware added to the chaos of their trestles, tools and hardware supplies.

While the painting proceeded, she decided to move beyond her brief and work on the small front garden. The area was tiny and neglected to the point that she decided a complete makeover was necessary. She could see it in her mind's eye — an enclosed courtyard that would screen the house from the street and provide an outdoor living area. She booked a reliable landscaper she knew and, worried about overspending, brought home the quote.

'It's up to you,' was all Philip said. 'If you decide it's necessary, go ahead.'

He might be present in body, but she knew his thoughts were with the babies who were in the last stages of preparation for surgery. He'd been offhand when she'd asked about his visit to his mother. 'When are you going to introduce us?' Perhaps he could invite Irene around for a meal. But he seemed put off by that suggestion.

'My mother has depression. She doesn't like strangers.'

'I should think company would be good for a person with depression.'

He must have realized how brusque he sounded. In a softer tone, he added, 'Actually, that's a very kind thought, Natalie. Let's arrange something, once I'm back in the land of the living.'

She nodded, reminding herself he was preoccupied with the risky surgery he was about to undertake. Thank God that would be over soon. He retreated into silence, and she left him to his journals and websites.

On the scheduled day, he went to the hospital at first light. He'd warned Natalie that he expected to be in theater with the twins till evening. The team was allowing up to twelve hours for the complex separation procedure. So few of these cases were ever encountered that even the most experienced surgeons had been double-checking their research.

Natalie was glad to head over to the cottage after breakfast and distract herself with hands-on work. Josh and his father started work by eight in the morning, when hammering and banging blended with the whine of sanding equipment and the cheerful beat of the radio in the van. She hadn't realized how much work would be needed to clear out the property. Even after they'd shifted the unwanted furniture, mattresses, and general junk, there were numerous bits and pieces that had accumulated over the course of decades. Len had been something of a hoarder. As Natalie sorted and discarded, she wondered what use he might have foreseen for lumps of driftwood, stones and shells that gathered dust on windowsills. The bags of unwearable clothing were set aside to possibly use as painting rags. But the cartons filled with old newspapers and magazines, and the strange collection of old bottles in one of the kitchen cupboards? She was careful not to touch the painting studio, as Philip had mentioned calling in an art appraiser to check out the stored canvases and assess their value.

Denise Courtney was keeping an eye on the changes, often arriving on the pretext of feeding Teddy in order to gather a progress report from Natalie. She didn't try to hide her interest in Len and his property. Why did she bother to come, carrying a cracked flowerpot and a tangled wind chime she'd retrieved from the heap of rubbish mounting up on the grass verge outside the gate? She held out her treasures with an embarrassed air.

'Would you mind if I took these as a

memento? A lick of paint is all they need.'

'Be my guest! Is there anything else you could use?'

'It's a silly sentimental thing, that's all. Len and I were friends for a long time.'

It was almost time for the men's morning break when they retreated to the porch with drinks and snacks they brought from home. As they set down their tools, Natalie turned to Denise. 'I'm going to put the kettle on. Why don't you join me?'

Denise needed no persuasion. Trailed by Teddy, who had adjusted to strangers on his territory and gauged when tidbits might be offered, she followed Natalie into the kitchen and looked around at the counters packed with half-sorted jars, bottles and food items. 'How can I help?'

Natalie laughed. 'A bomb might be the quickest way! Let's just take a break.'

Denise broke a biscuit into pieces

and offered them to Teddy. 'Len was fastidious about his art, but not much else. After his heart attack, he kept on painting. I think he sensed he hadn't much time left. Domestic things had to take care of themselves, and he allowed the wrong people to take advantage of him.'

She must be referring to men like that unsavory fellow who'd arrived as though he owned the place. Denise seemed to know a lot about her neighbor. She'd evidently been fond of him. Perhaps more than fond?

'It must have been hard for you, losing your husband when you were still young.' Natalie was thinking of her own mother and the struggle her life had been.

Denise nodded. 'Yes. You always think life's accidents and upsets are reserved for other people. Everything's rosy, and suddenly it's all snatched away from you. A sudden illness, and Jim was gone.'

It was like listening to her mother

describing the way Natalie's father had passed on so suddenly. 'How did you cope?'

Denise gave a resigned laugh. 'You don't. What does 'coping' mean? You go from one day to the next and you do what you have to do. One thing I did learn — if life is bloody awful, it generally improves. One day you start to notice the simple beauties again. You meet someone, you move, you're more understanding of other people and their troubles.'

'So you met Len?'

'I met Len.' The brief sentence held a world of nostalgia.

'And you fell in love?'

'Unfortunately, yes! But he was gay, as you young ones say.'

'So that's why he left his family! Philip was quite shocked when he heard about the inheritance. He'd been told his father cared nothing for him and was irresponsible.'

Denise was reflective as she set down her cup. 'Len? No, that's not true. I believe he never got over his troubles. I knew there'd been a woman in his life, though he never said he'd had a son. But he once showed me a set of drawings; said they weren't for sale or exhibition, and I could see why. They were full of grief. Do you know that religious image, Stabat Mater? The one that depicts Mary's pain as she stands at the foot of the cross, where her son hangs in his death throes? Len's drawings had the same impact on me. They portrayed a beautiful young woman, little more than a girl. His model, obviously. In some, she was holding a baby. Oh, the love in her gaze! But a man was leaving them. Hard to know why; perhaps going off to war or some distant job. He was grief-stricken. The woman had her back toward him, as though denying his existence. The despair on his face as he tore himself away was tragic. He knew he wouldn't see them again. I can tell you, those images were powerful. They made me weep.'

'I wonder what happened to them?' Natalie had guessed that some of Len's work might be hidden somewhere in the cottage, and had been meticulous in checking any drawers or boxes that might store his work. So far nothing had been uncovered except the rough studio canvases.

'Not long before he died, he gave them to me.'

'To you? Why?' Natalie hadn't meant to sound so disbelieving, but the idea of a famous painter handing over such personal images to his next-door neighbor seemed beyond belief.

'Because he trusted me, I suppose. I put them in the bank vault, like he asked.'

'What are you going to do with them?'

'Well, there's the rub! One day he handed me this folder, as casual as though it was the morning news. He asked me to take care of it, and to give it to the right person. Of course I asked him who that was, and he just said,

'You'll know.' He didn't want the pictures circulated while he was alive. Len was over-sensitive, like so many artists. He never really got over the way his life turned out. He was burdened with guilt, poor man, for something he couldn't help.'

'I honestly don't see what all the fuss was about. A person's sexuality is their own business.'

Denise's vivid blue eyes flashed with derision. 'These days, perhaps. There's the difference between your generation and mine, my dear. You have no idea how judgmental social attitudes used to be.' She dropped the last of the crumbs for Teddy and pushed back her chair. 'Now, the men are going back to work. I see you're getting along nicely with that good-looking young fellow.' Her eyes lit up with mischief, but if she was probing, Natalie had no intention of talking about Josh.

Just then he appeared at the door. 'Hi!' He offered a friendly wave to Denise. 'Nat, shall I chuck the old porch furniture? Teddy's chewed through half the cane. And the excavator's here.'

'Yes please, Josh. And I'd better go and show the driver what I want removed.' Natalie stood up, still digesting the confidences Denise had shared. *I met Len*. Such simple words, resonating with so many emotions — attraction, bonding, love, regret. For the first time, Natalie wondered whether her own mother had ever felt similar things after her husband had died so suddenly. Had she worked out her frustrations by tending to the pressing needs of all the lost or injured animals she sheltered? Like Denise, she must have known loneliness and wished she could meet a new partner to share life with. That thought simply hadn't occurred to Natalie. She felt ashamed of the stereotyped idea she'd had of the woman who had done her best to raise her little girl alone. As soon as she could, she would phone her mother.

Denise had provided an insight into Len McLeod, and Natalie needed to pass on the gist of that information to Philip. But that would have to wait. Right now he would be in theater, dealing with the unknown outcome of radical surgery.

She and Denise wandered back outside. The older woman collected the treasures she'd retrieved from the discards and stood watching as Josh strode past, casually balancing a large cane settee. Natalie, who was eyeing his tanned chest and broad shoulders, was startled when she heard Denise laugh softly. 'I see you appreciate the view! I should leave you to your work. See you again.' With a wave to Teddy, the older woman walked slowly back to her house.

★ ★ ★

Once the excavator started digging out the front yard, the cloud of dust made the men decide to pack up for the day. When Josh suggested taking Teddy down to the beach for some exercise, Natalie was tempted. The painter smelled of honest work and sunshine. That psychic camera was clicking again.

'I can't leave now,' she said. 'The driver asked for cash when he's done.'

'He's nearly finished. I'll board up that back window while we wait.'

As Josh walked away, Natalie looked around at the ravaged garden, and the extent of the renovation hit her. The property looked as though a cyclone had ripped through, destroying the yard and demolishing part of the house. At least no asbestos had been uncovered inside, and the only evidence of drug contamination had been the remains of a few dead marijuana plants, found in pots by Josh when he'd checked out the roof cavity.

It was all very well for Josh to reassure her that the results would be great. He didn't understand how hard it was to deal with Philip. Whenever she wanted to discuss the cottage, he brushed aside the topic as though it annoyed him. Perhaps he would be approachable after today. For better or for worse, the twins' fate would be known.

The driver deposited the last load of clay and rock in the tip truck and steered his excavator up the ramps. Its roar died and he slammed the tray. Natalie waited while he calculated his charge. The mounting bills were a worry. Philip might say he didn't care what she spent, but they had to deal with a reckoning soon. What if she'd overstepped his brief?

Her mind flashed back to the previous evening. Philip had been intent on studying some specialist medical website he subscribed to. He'd hardly spoken to her. In bed she'd slipped her arm across his back, wanting to cuddle, but he'd been asleep within a minute. And she felt tears fill her eyes as she had an intuition they were on the verge of breaking up. Oh, she'd parted ways with other boyfriends, but never with this feeling of sick dread, as though she was losing something precious.

From the beginning, Natalie had admired Philip's dedication, his intellect, his determination to woo her into moving in with him. He'd seemed far above her then. But now that she'd come to know him better, she'd discovered he was a complex man with many problems he did not want to share. She had no idea how to get past his barriers or figure out what she really wanted. Neither of them had spoken of love. Could she be in love with such a defensive, prickly man? She knew he appreciated her beauty and youth, but there were umpteen young, beautiful women in the world. Why her?

She'd had an impulse to shake him awake and confront him with her questions. Instead she'd stared into the darkness, telling herself that he needed his sleep. This was the crucial day. He deserved peace of mind. Until the surgery was over, she would simply have to be patient.

Natalie paid the driver and tucked the receipt in her pocket. She was determined to account for every dollar of the outlay. So far money had never been raised as an issue between them, but she remembered a few past boyfriends with whom finance had become an ugly bone of contention.

When Josh returned, she was still unsure whether to take up his offer. Instinct warned her that outings with him were a mistake. Sure, he knew she was in a relationship, and his actions had been purely friendly. But she should step back. It was too easy to relax and laugh and enjoy his easy chat. He didn't bother to hide the admiration she saw whenever they made eye contact. If he made a pass, would she be tempted?

She was about to turn down his invitation when Teddy decided the matter. He'd been watching disapprovingly from the porch as machinery rumbled all over his territory. Now he crossed the churned dirt and dropped his lead at Natalie's feet, his curly tail quivering in an attempt at a wag. Josh squatted to pat him, glancing up at Natalie with a beguiling grin. 'He's begging for a walk.'

152

How could she refuse? 'Okay. I'll lock up.'

Leaving her car parked at the cottage, Natalie bent to hoist Teddy into the front of the van. Sensing that Josh was giving her legs an appreciative glance, she climbed into the front seat, primly tugging her short skirt over her thighs. As he drove, his hand on the gear console was only inches away from her knee. Why did she feel a flicker of desire? They were only going for a quick walk, for heaven's sake!

Teddy was scrabbling to reach the window, his sharp claws digging at the seat. He was a muscular little dog, determined to have his way. Natalie plumped him firmly on her lap, caressing his soft fur until he settled.

'You're growing attached to him.' Josh had noticed her affection. 'Why don't you take him home?'

'I don't think animals are allowed at the apartment.' Even if they were, she doubted Philip would agree to have a pet. Would Teddy never find a loving home again? She remembered the story of Greyfriars Bobby, a Skye Terrier in Scotland who, fed by the community, had guarded his master's grave for fourteen years until he died of old age. Would that be Teddy's fate?

In a few minutes, Josh pulled up near the lake. Yachts, catamarans and launches rocked gently at anchor. Natalie's plans for the renovated cottage were to reflect its seaside environment; but the still water, a neutral color that was neither grey nor blue, would be difficult to match in paint or fabric. Maybe curtains patterned to suggest the shadows of vertical masts wavering on the lapping surface . . .

Teddy scratched on the window, whining as he eyed a cluster of pelicans waiting for fishermen's leftovers near the gutting table. 'You'd better not run away.' She opened the door. Like any normal dog free to chase a target, he rocketed onto the sand, sending the large birds scattering in cumbersome flight. Teddy diverted to a group of seagulls. Enraged squawks changed his pace to a gallop as he bounced along the sand.

Josh laughed and set out in pursuit, Natalie racing to catch up. She bent and picked up a stick, calling the dog as she tossed it high above the tide-line. Teddy halted. Diverting to this new game, he set off to retrieve it. Natalie's gaze followed the arching stick. It seemed frozen in mid-air. Her surroundings had blurred and there was a simmering hum like a thousand bees buzzing in her ears. She sat down on a handy bench and blinked, trying to clear her vision. She couldn't think. Her mind was a blank.

Not aware of her odd state, Josh was chatting. 'Funny to think the old guy probably sat right here, sketching the boats . . . Hey! Are you okay?' He'd noticed her lapse and was looking down at her, his face inquiring.

She nodded. Oh yes, they were at the beach. She couldn't remember coming here, but there was Teddy, excitedly running from one scent to another.

'Did you bring me here?' Now she had a vague memory. They'd been at the cottage. It was all coming back.

'What's going on, Natalie? You sound kind of strange.'

She tried to reassure him. 'I'm fine. I'll just sit here for a few minutes.'

'Too much sun, you reckon?'

'Maybe. Or some virus.' She did have a headache, and her arm was tingling, as though she'd had a mild electric shock. She didn't want to talk; it was hard getting the words out. She remembered that similar episode when she'd been driving back from Sydney. This would wear off just as quickly. She needed to reassure Josh; she didn't want any fuss. She was never sick.

'Take Teddy for his run,' she insisted. 'Just give me five minutes. I've had this once before. It goes away.'

'I'm taking you back to the cottage.' He sounded definite. 'I'll round up Teddy. You wait here.'

Slowly Natalie made her way back to the vehicle. She must have pushed herself too hard. The past week had been strenuous as she joined in the demolition work, lifting and carrying heavy loads alongside the men. She rested her head on the seat and waited for Josh and Teddy.

'Feeling okay now?' It was a relief to hear his voice. If she'd been alone, she might have found it hard to make her way home. She was glad he took care of the driving, and he insisted on making her a cup of tea when they reached the cottage. 'Reckon you should see a doctor.' He handed her the cup.

She smiled. 'I live with a doctor.'

'So you say. Do you have a regular GP?'

'I'm the healthiest person on the planet!' She picked up regular prescriptions for the pill; otherwise she steered clear of doctors.

'You need to get checked.' He sounded masterful.

'Stop nagging me. I'm fine.'

'Promise!' It was an order.

'Okay!'

'And tell your boyfriend. He ought to know.'

She had no intention of dragging Philip into it. He would be unavailable; and even if he checked a text message during a break, what could she say? His work provided all the medical problems he could handle, especially today. The last thing he needed was a complaining partner.

'Reckon you'll be able to drive home? I could — '

'I said I'm fine.' She sounded cranky, but Josh was overdoing the concern. She'd had a bit too much sun, that was all.

Together they locked up the cottage. Anticipating they were leaving, Teddy lay down with a heavy sigh, nose resting on his paws. As Natalie prepared to drive off, Josh surprised her, reaching through her car window to gently brush a dark curl off her forehead.

'You need someone to look after you, Nat.'

'Who? You, Prince Charming?'

He just grinned. 'Try me and see.'

'Oh, go home! See you tomorrow.'

But a smile lingered on her lips as she started the car. She was an independent woman, but being nurtured wasn't unwelcome. Today of all days, Philip was unavailable. While she was driving, at least he must have availed himself of a short break to phone her. The brief message went to voice mail, but when she was able to access it he sounded upbeat. The surgery must be going well. She planned a quiet night. If he came home at all, he would be late.

Natalie had almost forgotten that strange turn on the beach, until she had another episode in the shower that night. By now she recognized the oncoming symptoms and darted from under the hot water, grabbing a towel before she sank down on the bathroom stool. The room tilted, tingling reached her fingers, and her mind blanked out. Instinct kept her seated, clutching the towel around her shoulders. The hum of running water thundered like a rainstorm.

When she came to, she was shivering — whether from cold or fear she didn't know. Something was wrong with her. Josh was right; she needed to see her doctor, even if this was only some virus. Slowly she dried herself and pulled on her nightwear. She hadn't heard again from Philip when she went to bed.

7

His side of the bed hadn't been slept in when she awoke. She found he'd sent a text, explaining he would stay at the hospital overnight. So at least the babies must have survived their ordeal. She felt a surge of relief for them, and for Philip and the others in the surgical team. She couldn't imagine carrying such a tremendous responsibility; the worst that could go wrong with her work was a dissatisfied client or an unpaid invoice. Philip's job involved life or death. No wonder he withdrew into himself.

In a way, his absence was a blessing this morning. Natalie was dreading her visit to her doctor and certainly wasn't inclined to listen to gory medical accounts of the twins' operation. Really, she didn't want to discuss her fears with anybody until she had the facts.

She acknowledged Philip's text; then, with a feeling of dread, called her doctor's surgery. After describing her symptoms to the receptionist, she was fitted in for an appointment the same afternoon. To kill the hours of waiting, she cleaned the apartment, made out a grocery list and watched a morning show on TV until it was time to go.

She checked in at the desk and was asked to sit in the waiting room, where babies wailed and patients coughed and spluttered with late-winter ailments. Natalie flicked the pages of a magazine, but the gossip about celebrity break-ups and baby bumps bored her. She read the posters on the walls. They pointed out myriad ailments she should be tested for or vaccinated against. What a morbid atmosphere! These places gave her the creeps! How could Philip choose to spend his working life with sick people?

A bent old man pushing a wheeling frame shuffled out of Doctor Bidwell's consulting room. After a minute, the physician came to the door, beckoning Natalie. She went with slow footsteps to explain the reason for her visit. Her doctor listened carefully. He took her blood pressure and decided to run an ECG. She climbed onto a narrow bed, where a practice nurse attached leads to her chest and ran the test. Dr. Bidwell examined the paper strip with its cryptic tracings and said it looked normal. She wanted to say 'I could have told you that'. Perhaps he didn't know what was wrong with her. She felt hopeful. It was probably just some virus, as she'd guessed.

'Just run through your symptoms again,' he suggested, scribbling notes on her file and standing up as she talked. 'I want to run a few neurological tests. Would you walk in a straight line to the door and back?'

After she did so, easily, he asked her to follow the movement of his finger as he waved it from side to side. He picked up a small rubber hammer and tapped her knee and ankle joints while she sat with bad grace, wishing he'd stop wasting time.

'That all seems normal.'

As the doctor typed into the computer, Natalie stared at the décor. Boy, did he need a consultant in here! Not a cushion, rug or flower in sight. On the floor there was a set of scales and a model of a skeleton. A skull and an upside-down baby in a dissected plastic pelvis decorated his bookshelf, and his desk was taken up with blood-pressure equipment, medical tomes, and a printer now spitting out several laboratory forms. He was handing them to her.

'This is for general blood work. And this is for a CT scan.'

'A scan? Is that really necessary?' What a fuss! Today Natalie felt perfectly normal, and resented wasting time and money when she could be choosing paint colors and curtain material.

Her heart plummeted further when he added, 'You may need an MRI as well. We'll see what shows up.'

'So you do think something's wrong with me?'

'Your symptoms could suggest a TIA. Temporary ischemic attack. That's a blockage to an artery supplying the brain. It can precede a full-blown stroke.'

How could he sound so matter-of-fact? 'What? I thought only old people had strokes!'

'No. They can strike a teenager, even a baby. I'm not saying that's what's going on, but we need to rule out any serious problems.'

Did he think a smile would reassure her? She prided herself on her excellent health; had even boasted of it to Philip, telling him she'd never need his attention in that capacity. But the doctor was rattling off a list while she listened in horror: stroke, brain tumor, neurological disease . . . She searched for words, found none, and remained silent. This couldn't be real. It was some damn bug. She stood, taking the forms he'd given her.

'There's a laboratory that has this equipment in the mall. Get yourself over there. You shouldn't have too long a wait.' He had an afterthought. 'By the way, Natalie, you shouldn't be taking the pill until we clear up this issue. It's been associated with clotting problems. And get onto aspirin, one hundred milligrams daily. Any chemist carries it.'

And with that, he politely ushered her to the door. She paid at the desk and stepped out into the sunny mall. The world had changed as she walked in the direction of the medical laboratory. Brightly colored parrots squabbled in one of the eucalyptus trees, turning the canopy into a frenzy of noise. Everybody was rushing, while she felt she'd walked into a solid wall.

She'd thought she had all the time in the world to make plans, change partners, pick and choose . . . and, sometime in the future, decide on a settled plan. But everything she knew about life was wrong. She might not have much time at all. Everywhere she saw symbols of life's pleasures, about to be snatched away from her. Suits and evening frocks stored in plastic film hung in the dry-cleaner's doorway like hopeful partners meeting on the dance floor. Hadn't she once viewed *Dancing with the Stars* on television, imagining herself in one of those glamorous dresses and planning to enroll in a Latin ballroom course one day? Why hadn't she bothered? People sat at tables outside the patisserie and she thought of all the times she'd eyed those delectable cakes and walked on by, thinking of her figure. She should have stuffed her face! Tomorrow she might be in a hospital, or worse. She was only twenty-six.

With a pang of longing, she felt the warm sunshine and registered the gentle breeze caressing her skin. Was this the meaning of a wake-up call? To dance, to eat, to see the beauty of trees and birds . . . Such simple gifts suddenly filled her with a yearning that she'd wasted so many opportunities. Around her, elderly people made up a good percentage of the shoppers. Their slow pace as they hobbled and limped used to annoy her, but now she stood aside, allowing them time. A teenager scooted past her in a wheelchair, giving her a cute smile and a wave. How could life be so cruel to the young? Was she another victim about to be snatched away in her prime? Oh, she had to be healthy, to be well.

The medical laboratory collected her blood sample and booked her in for a scan. Apparently Dr. Bidwell had marked the form as 'urgent'. She decided she would avoid telling Philip until she knew the facts. He would be preoccupied during the critical post-surgery days, and talking about the doctor's speculations would make them real. Surely this whole scare was due to a virus.

Natalie remembered she was supposed to buy groceries. But the idea of walking along aisles, picking up meat and vegetables, was just too ludicrous at the moment. She needed to be home. She needed Philip to hold her and tell her everything would be all right. Why wasn't he there? She had a crazy impulse to drive to the hospital and beg to see him. No, surely he must be coming home soon. He'd been there for over thirty hours. She'd text him again, and find out what time he'd be back.

Natalie stood in a doorway and tapped in a quick message. She ought to withdraw some money from the ATM, but her legs were shaky. Stepping off the pavement, she almost walked in front of a moving car. The blare of its horn shattered her last vestige of self-control. Bursting into tears, she found her car and huddled in the driver's seat, wanting to hide away from the rest of the world.

★   ★   ★

Somehow, she was able to fill the next days with a semblance of routine. Philip was so busy working overtime as he monitored the babies' progress that they barely spent any time together. He was constantly coming and going, while

Natalie went on with her work at the cottage. What was the point of brooding? She'd had the scan and would see the doctor again as soon as the results came through.

Besides, intimacy would only raise more problems. She'd stopped taking the pill, and knew she couldn't take any risks until she was on alternative birth control. But an underlying fear sent her to the internet, where she browsed a host of awful complications and diseases. Too much information!

When Josh asked her what the doctor had said, she snapped at him: 'Stop hassling me! When I know if there's anything wrong, I'll tell you.' She didn't want sympathy. The only creature she felt close to was Teddy. He was becoming attached to her, as Josh had pointed out. He would race to greet her; his short, curly tail twitching like a flag as he pawed her legs and did his little dervish dance. The feel of his warm, muscular body, so full of life despite his dilemma, somehow made her feel that her problems could be overcome. If only she could take him back to Philip's! Visualizing the look on his face, she sighed. He'd already told her he didn't see the point of pets. To him, they represented extra work, responsibility and health problems.

But her efforts at distraction failed on the evening before she was due at the surgery to hear the results of her tests. With a sick feeling in her stomach and knotted nerves, she was really trying to keep busy, running a load of laundry and wiping out the fridge. Philip, who was home for the evening, caught her hand as she went to check the washing machine. 'You're a hive of industry! Come and sit with me.' She pulled away. Was he lining up to have sex? She'd already turned him down last night, saying she wasn't in the mood. Of course Philip didn't know her doctor had told her to go off the pill. She felt her last reserves of courage drain away.

'In a minute. I'm just going to have a shower.' She escaped to the bathroom, turning her body from side to side under the soothing jet of warm water. She tipped her head back and allowed rivulets to caress her scalp. The steamy cubicle insulated her from the world as she massaged in shampoo, rinsed and combed a generous dollop of conditioner through her hair. Philip took three-minute showers, assuring her nobody needed longer to soap and rinse, but he clearly didn't understand the therapeutic effect of warm running water.

Reluctantly, after ten minutes, she checked to see that the cap was tight on the designer body wash, switched off the water and stepped out into the embrace of a large, soft towel. Such nice things! The towels of her childhood had been rags, scratchy and thin, and probably used on animals and humans alike. Drying off her dripping hair, she pulled on a monogrammed bath robe and went back downstairs.

'Feeling better?' Philip patted his knee. 'Come here, I want to ask you something.'

Apprehension surged through Natalie's body. Now what? All she wanted was to get into bed, pull up the covers, and try to forget that tomorrow she had a doctor's appointment to get the results of her tests. She perched awkwardly on his knee.

'I was emptying the trash for the pick-up in the morning,' he said. 'I found these.' He sounded calm but his tone made her wonder. 'Natalie, by any chance are you pregnant?'

She was shocked. 'Of course not! Why would you think that?'

Taking a pill pack from his pocket, he indicated the half-used tablets. 'Because you're throwing out your pills. And last night you turned your back on me.'

So he hadn't believed her feeble excuse of a headache. 'I'm not pregnant, Philip,' she assured him in a soft voice, 'but I do need to tell you something.' And clinging to him like a little girl, she burst into tears, allowing all her doubts and fears to spill out while he listened attentively, stroking her hair.

'You've been worried about this all week. Why didn't you tell me, Natalie?'

Her face was pressed against his chest. She could feel his heartbeat, strong and steady. 'I was waiting until I had the results.' She didn't remind him how preoccupied he'd been. Perhaps it had suited her to face her problem alone. Why spoil things? She knew Philip had chosen her as his antidote to the sickness and suffering he dealt with every working day. She brought beauty into his surroundings. She could guess the consequences if she turned out to be just another patient, stuck in a hospital bed, stricken with illness. Oh, she just couldn't be sick! Denial had got her through the last few days, and she simply hadn't felt ready to repeat all the awful possibilities the doctor and the internet suggested.

But her fear was replaced by a sense of safety as Philip's hands gently lifted her face to meet his gaze. His green eyes reflected genuine concern. Comforted, she nestled against him. He was a doctor. Surely he'd know what to do for the best outcome.

'Sweetheart, please — tell me why you needed a scan.'

So she tried to extract facts from the jumble of terror in her mind. Fear of her body's failure. Fear of hospitals and surgery. Fear of losing Philip. She imagined herself crippled by a stroke or damaged by brain surgery. They would shave her head. She would be hideous. Taking a shuddering breath, she spilled out her jumbled thoughts, dreading his reaction.

But something amazing was happening. In the midst of her outburst, he'd called her 'sweetheart'. He was holding her as though she was a treasure. Philip wasn't a man for endearments. In their months together, they'd never strayed into romance. It was a given that they were a couple, a duo, two people who found each other attractive. But she wasn't allowing for that buried compassion; that selfless caring she'd seen him pour out on his patients. It seemed her

175

problem had given him access to the
tenderness she so desperately needed
now.

He pulled her close, warming her,
gently stroking her as one would soothe
a pet. His touch felt protective. 'Why
didn't you tell me? Why go through this
alone?'

'I didn't want to worry you.' But that
wasn't strictly fair. She had to own her
own insecurity. Deep down, she believed
that it was only her looks that attracted
men, and her talents they admired.

'Worry me?' He sounded incredulous.
'I cherish you, Natalie. That means I
want to share everything. Not just the
good parts.'

He cherished her. But what exactly
did he mean? He'd never said he loved
her. Never, even in the heights of passion
or its aftermath. All this time, had she
mistaken the agenda by playing sexual
games, taking control, acting out the
artistic and independent woman she'd
thought he admired? All the time she'd
accessorized herself for him, taken over

the renovations, decorated his apartment, she'd just assumed that was her role. Yet it was only now, at her weakest, that he was holding her close, saying he cherished her . . .

No, he couldn't be talking of love, any more than she had ever used the word, in this relationship or previous ones. She couldn't expect it now. But it felt so good leaning on him, letting him comfort her. And when he insisted he would take her to the doctor and be with her while the diagnosis was decided, she just nodded, nestling her tangled hair against his chest and not caring when her tears flowed.

★　★　★

Natalie's appointment was scheduled for mid-morning. While she brewed coffee and made toast, Philip telephoned the hospital. She heard him cancel his day's work.

'Are you sure you can leave the twins?'

'Natalie, I'm coming with you, and that's decided. The rest of the team are available.' He was adamant. It was only when he'd parked the Lexus and was walking beside her into the surgery that she realized just how grateful she felt, knowing he was with her. Her stomach was clenched in a hard knot and her lips felt dry.

The people waiting to be called sat in silence, reading old magazines, flicking the pages without interest or staring into space. Were they harboring invisible diseases too? A child coughed, his flushed face crumpled in misery. Philip reached over and held her hand.

When Natalie was called in, she introduced Philip, who took a back seat, waiting quietly for the GP to discuss the results of the tests. As the doctor clipped a film onto a lighted overhead and scanned a pathology report, she sat rigidly, staring at the model baby forever locked head-down in its plastic prison.

Dr. Bidwell offered a smile she took to be encouraging. 'Your blood work is quite normal, and as far as I can tell, you're not about to have a stroke. Nor is there any form of tumor showing. However . . . ' He indicated a small arrowed blob on the scan. 'This is where the trouble's occurring.' Although Philip leaned forward and closely examined the area, he remained silent, allowing Natalie to follow the doctor's words. 'There's an abnormality here. We call it an AVM, or arteriovenous malformation. Probably been there since birth. It's a tangle of tiny blood vessels, and that slight bulge indicates a weakened point.'

'Might it burst? How would I know?'

'Believe me, you'd know.' The doctor's expression was serious. 'That might never happen. One doesn't get warning. However, I consider your best course is to have it surgically repaired. It's a delicate procedure, but we have excellent neurosurgeons locally.'

'So that's why I've had those odd symptoms?'

The doctor hesitated. 'Look, it's

unusual. For all we know, you could have picked up some kind of virus. It's only by chance that this condition has showed up on the scan. The thing is, you know about it now. It's your decision.'

'My partner will help me decide.' She turned to Philip. 'He's the surgeon who operated on those twins.' She did not hide the admiration in her words.

Dr. Bidwell glanced with respect at Philip. 'Then you are certainly in good hands to get the right advice.'

'How would I go about getting this treated?' Natalie's mind was spinning, this time with dread.

'I can give you a referral to the hospital.' He began writing on an official-looking form. As she took the envelope, he offered an encouraging smile. 'Natalie, it's fortunate we've spotted this before it can cause real trouble. Once it's repaired, I assure you, life will go back to normal. You'll have some rehabilitation, because the brain can take time to settle down after surgery. But I don't expect any long-term problems. You'll be as good as new.'

The interview was almost over. Philip still hadn't intervened, though she knew he'd paid close attention to everything that had taken place.

'By the way, you did heed my advice about the pill? We can look at some alternative; a diaphragm, perhaps?'

Natalie's mind was blank. How could she think about sex, or babies, after what he'd just told her?

Philip stood up, offering Dr. Bidwell a decisive handshake. 'We'll chat about that later.' She was glad he'd taken control. He would know what to do, about everything. She clung to that thought as they walked out into the sunshine, his arm protectively around her shoulders.

★   ★   ★

'Would you like to have a coffee?' Philip offered. They were passing a café, the social hub where the hurrying people

181

with their strollers and shopping carts stopped to relax and chat. Natalie looked pale. Maybe a cappuccino would pick her up.

She squeezed his hand, acknowledging the offer. 'No, thanks. I'd rather go home.'

She hardly spoke a word as Philip drove her back to the apartment. He'd delivered enough bad news in his role as a surgeon to be familiar with shock. She sat on the couch like a statue, letting him wait on her as he fixed sandwiches and coffee. She needed to discuss the issue, but he would leave that for her to raise. To distract her, he flicked on the midday news — the usual assortment of stabbings, home invasions, arrests and death.

Natalie watched for a few minutes before she stood up and switched off the set. 'I suppose we should talk.'

'Whenever you're ready.'

'I'm thinking Dr. Bidwell might be an alarmist. An operation seems pretty drastic. I mean, I've probably been walking around since birth with this condition. I've had a couple of funny episodes, but really, I'm perfectly okay now.'

He understood why she was trying to fool herself. Denial was a common psychological process. Some patients grasped at straws, and the worse their condition, the more they were inclined to resort to alternative remedies or fancy diets. But no herb or diet was going to fix Natalie's problem. Unless it was surgically repaired, she would never feel safe. In the back of her mind she would be watching and waiting, wondering if and when the AVM would rupture. It was a very real possibility. The thought of losing her slammed him like a blow to the chest. But he had to let it be her decision. All he could offer was his support during her time of preparation and waiting.

'What do you think, Philip? Is the operation as safe as the doctor implied?'

Philip hesitated. All surgery carried risk, and invading the brain was a delicate and specialized process. Yet, in his opinion, she had no choice. And the recovery rate for an AVM repair was very high.

'The operation is safe.' She needed reassurance. But still she looked uncertain.

'And you think I should have it?' She was ready with her next question even as he nodded. 'Will you do it?'

Natalie's trust pierced his heart. Clearly she had complete faith in his skill. In reality, however, she had no proof of his ability as a surgeon, but was willing to place herself in his hands and give him access to the most intimate organ in her body. 'Sweetheart, I'm your partner. The hospital wouldn't allow it.'

'But you've just done far more complicated surgery on those babies.'

She looked vulnerable. Her careless tumble of dark curls framed her pale face. He saw soulful reproach in her gaze and caressed her cold hand. 'That was different. I wasn't emotionally involved.'

'Are you saying you are, with me?'

Didn't she believe him? 'Of course I'm involved with you! We live together! We sleep together, don't we?'

She fell silent, but her expression was doubtful. So it might be true that he'd never verbalized the slightest commitment to a long-term future with her, but quite frankly it was Natalie's own attitude that kept him at arm's length. She'd made a point of telling him how highly she valued her independence. And he could understand. She'd explained how, right from the ages of nine or ten, she'd resented the way her mother's life was so restricted as a single parent, short of money and tied to all those needy animals. Philip understood all too well the power of childhood lessons. In their different ways, both he and Natalie had come to exactly the same conclusion as children. Life had to offer more, and they would study, and work, and take the dues they'd been deprived of, growing up in hardship, without fathers. But this crisis was changing everything. What

185

was going through her head?

'I just want you there.'

'I will be there. Just not in the operating room. The surgeon I'm thinking of is very capable. I'd trust him if I had to undergo the procedure.'

'Will I have a long wait?'

Did she have health insurance? Unlikely. She'd boasted several times that she had never been sick. Perhaps he could pull a few strings at the hospital. 'Here's what I suggest. We'll follow up on your referral, get any further tests that are needed, and I'll have a word with my colleague.' She seemed satisfied with that plan. The waiting period would be hard, and he resolved to arrange some time off work. They could plan a few relaxing days, perhaps take a weekend away. He didn't want her working on the cottage. Better to call a halt to further work for now. He expected her to come with him to speak to Josh and his father, but she suggested he should go alone.

'I don't want people talking about

me,' she said. 'Just pay them for the work so far and tell them we're unavailable for a while. Say we're going away. Anything.'

Philip didn't understand this phobia about hospitals and illness. Was she trying to pretend nothing was wrong? Would the men resent being pulled off the job? He wasn't even sure what stage the renovations had reached. Work had taken all his energy recently. He'd left everything to her, and now he felt a twinge of guilt. The least he could do was handle this temporary setback and provide the tradesmen with the changed timetable. If Natalie had her surgery within a fortnight, she would need at least a month's recovery time. Brain surgery had unpredictable symptoms. She could expect headaches, tiredness, and mood changes. She'd be irritable and emotional as her body readjusted. But she didn't need to hear this kind of talk yet.

After lunch, he left her for a few hours and went to the hospital to rearrange his roster and speak with his colleague. Bryan Mason was a brain surgeon he'd worked with on several cases. Philip explained Natalie's condition and showed Bryan the referral and imaging films. It was agreed that his colleague would see her, order an MRI, and settle on a date for surgery. Sometimes it helped to know the right people, though whether Natalie would appreciate his intervention remained to be seen. Yet he had noticed a change in her. As she leaned on him, needing his support, he realized just how much energy she usually exerted to prove she was independent. But now that she needed it, he would do whatever he could to support her through her ordeal.

★ ★ ★

In the morning, Philip arrived at the cottage under a leaden sky that promised heavy rain. He parked behind a pick-up truck and waited while a council worker loaded the last of the discarded furniture and building materials lying on the verge. It was hard to believe the dilapidated dwelling had housed so many unwanted things. Len McLeod's life lay there — decades of gathered objects, touched by his father's hands, now tossed out as rubbish. Nothing looked to be of any value. Was this clutter the sum total of a man's life? Apparently the painter had placed no worth on the material world, except in his art.

Curiosity had sent Philip to search the internet and read up on his father. Len held a significant CV in the artists' community, dating back several decades to the present. His canvases were hung in several galleries; he'd held exhibitions and been awarded more than one major prize. Painting had remained his life's work. A scholarship had allowed him to make one overseas trip to the main European art destinations, back in the '80s. Otherwise he seemed to have been a solitary man, content to live in this backwater, immune to the family and friendly ties most people build during their lifetime.

With a vicious heave, the council worker hoisted the last of the furniture aboard his vehicle. Shaking his head at the assumptions of people who had money, he strolled over to the Lexus and tapped on the window. 'Your load exceeds regulations. You're lucky I haven't picked up much else or I'd have left you to pay a private carrier to move your stuff.' With that, he drove off.

Philip stepped out and picked his way across the uneven ground where a bulldozer had recently left tracks. Hearing a bark, he saw a movement on the porch. That dog he'd seen weeks ago was still hanging around. He wondered why Natalie hadn't contacted the RSPCA to take it away. It shouldn't be living like this, skulking and hiding, poor creature. Now it was coming toward him, wagging its curl of a tail.

'Hello, boy,' he said diffidently. He'd never had anything to do with animals, but its lonely plight tugged at his heart. Strays had been unwelcome in the rental properties of his childhood. His mother had warned him not to touch the mangy cats that fought and mated outside his window, or the skinny dogs that hunted for food scraps. As an adult, his caution had been confirmed when he had to perform surgery on a small child who had been badly bitten in a dog attack.

But this creature seemed friendly; in fact, was greeting him like a long-lost friend, giving excited yips and even spinning around in circles. Philip laughed. The *joie de vivre* of the little dog was contagious. He looked well fed, his short coat was brushed, and his eyes were bright. Someone was tending to his needs — presumably the lady from next door. She seemed a decent enough woman, if a chatterbox, sharing the hopes and disappointments of her love life as though Philip was a close friend.

The information that Len was homosexual hadn't greatly surprised him. These days, sexual preference was a non-issue among his peers. What people did in their private life was their business. Philip wasn't interested in the dalliances of men and women who were now either dead or about ready to go into a retirement home. His father's sexual makeup had nothing to do with why Len hadn't taken steps to meet his son. He'd left it a bit late to include Philip in his life. His mother would nurse her hurt for the rest of her life. And inheriting this dump was hardly compensation for his fatherless childhood.

The dog trotting at his heels, he explored the back yard, then used his key to open the house and did a quick inspection of the work to date. The rooms seemed bigger without all their clutter. Natalie must have worked hard, and the two handymen had made progress, replacing Len's amateur carpentry and lining the walls with new plasterboard, ready for its fresh paint and wallpaper. The studio was as he'd seen it before, and Philip remembered he must arrange for the art appraiser to come and do his valuation. Deciding to phone the tradesmen and explain the temporary delay, he locked up, intending to go home, but the dog had other ideas.

'You've got me confused with someone else, mate.'

The animal seemed absolutely convinced he had found his master. Perhaps he wanted a walk? There was a leash hanging over the porch railing. Feeling oddly flattered by the dog's attention, he attached the clip to his collar. A worn nametag read 'Teddy'. What a name to inflict on a dog!

He lifted the dog into the back of the Lexus, tying the leash to stop him jumping up on the leather upholstery. He'd stretch his legs with a quick walk along the beach before the weather broke. The lake was only a five-minute drive away.

As he parked, a brisk wind was whipping the waves to whitecaps, and moored craft rocked from side to side. The impending storm was bringing fishermen back to shore. Philip watched a couple of boaties who were efficiently winching a luxury cruiser up the launching ramp. Another sailor was hooking up his trailer, and further out, a solitary man was steering for the ramp, his small outboard motor sending out a steady throb.

Philip untied Teddy. Grabbing the end of the lead, he prepared to set out for a walk in the bracing wind. Teddy seemed distracted by the myriad sounds and scents. Sniffing attentively, he fixed his bulbous gaze on the incoming boat. He listened intently, then suddenly tugged hard enough to slip his collar, and raced on his stubby legs toward the water. The lead dangling from his hand, Philip ran after him, pulling up short as he reached the waterline.

Could dogs swim? It seemed so. Teddy was heading out to the small boat, bobbing up and down amid the whitecaps. Philip called him several times, with growing anxiety. The dog wasn't responding at all to his shouts. Did he have the brains to understand he must turn around and come back to safety?

The incoming boat was almost at the ramp, but Teddy had failed to overtake it and instead forged straight ahead, heading for the horizon now. Philip began to panic. What was he supposed to do? He wasn't much of a swimmer. There were a few dilapidated wooden boats lying sideways on the grass, but even if he borrowed one, he didn't know how to row.

The gentle waters of the lake now contained an ominous darkness. Philip tried desperately to fix Teddy in his sights, but the dog's form was growing smaller. Was that his head, or just another wave? Unless Philip acted now, the dog was going to drown.

Driven by growing panic, he jogged toward the man who had just arrived at the ramp and was preparing to tie up and fetch his trailer. 'Can you help? My dog's out there.'

The young man responded at once. 'No worries, mate! Hop in.' He was very like Josh — about the same age, and with the same easy manner.

Forgetting his tailored trousers and dress shoes, Philip waded out to the craft and gratefully scrambled aboard with the boatie's help. The outboard fired and the craft was steering back out to sea.

'Where is he?'

Philip scanned the water, but visibility was hazy now as spray flew off the cresting waves. The boat bumped over the uneven surface, jolting its passengers.

'See him anywhere?'

'Not yet. I've lost my bearings. I think he was trying to get to your boat, then he headed straight out.'

'Bit rough to take your dog swimming.' The young fellow grinned.

'He's not mine. Is that something, over there?'

'Sorry, mate. Just waves.'

As though hoping for a miracle, Philip gazed back to shore, which was bereft of human life, as the storm broke. Overhead, jagged strands of lightning lit up the bruised sky. A few seconds later, thunder rumbled violently, as though accompanying the drama playing out below.

Philip felt as bad as if he was losing a patient on the operating table. This was his fault. He should have realized. Len must have often taken Teddy out in his old runabout. And now, mistakenly pursuing his master, it seemed Teddy's quest had failed. The faithful dog had drowned. How could a casual moment of impulse turn to tragedy?

Natalie must feel as he did, alone and spiraling down into a helpless vortex. What would she think of him when he admitted what had happened?

'Hang on!' The boatie squinted, peering into the haze. He swung the tiller, the boat taking water as waves slopped against the sides. 'What's that?' A floating object, just visible, was bobbing up and down ahead.

Philip felt a surge of hope. 'I think that's him!'

The boatie grinned. 'Then let's go get him.' He revved up the outboard motor and headed toward Teddy, who was by now exhausted and struggling to stay afloat.

Not caring about his clothes, Philip fell on his knees in the waterlogged boat and reached over to haul Teddy aboard. The animal, with the extreme strength of fear, struggled until Philip nearly overbalanced. The boatie came to his aid and together they dragged Teddy aboard, where he shook himself violently and began to lick Philip with passionate intensity.

'Your little mate's glad to see you.' The boatie grinned again as he headed the boat back to shore. Overhead, the display of forked lightning intensified, and the thunderclaps rumbled around the bay as though Zeus himself was celebrating the lucky rescue.

Philip fiddled with the collar and leash, securing it firmly to Teddy. He had learned a hard lesson, and it would be a while before his anxiety settled. Teddy, however, seemed to have forgotten his ordeal already. Once he was back on solid ground he prepared to set off again along the sand, where birds had landed to shelter from the approaching storm. But it wasn't the time for an excursion. Philip's trousers clung unpleasantly to his legs and his shoes were wet. After thanking his rescuer again, he marched the dog to his car and tipped him onto the back seat, in no state to worry about marks on his pristine upholstery.

As he made the short journey to the cottage, Philip worried about Teddy. The ordeal had forged an unexpected bond between him and the ownerless pet. The dog's near-drowning had aroused such strong emotions in Philip that now he felt responsible for his wellbeing. A downpour was brewing, and the animal was already shivering and wet. He couldn't just dump him on the porch and leave. Then he remembered the neighbour, Denise — she'd said she was looking after Len's dog. He should at least check that she was home.

He opened the back door of the Lexus, flinching at the sandy footprints and streaks of dirt on his immaculate leather upholstery. This dog was worse than a toddler. Why did people saddle themselves with such unpredictable creatures? His clothes were ruined, his car was stained, and all the bedraggled animal wanted to do was to investigate some unmentionable deposit on the road. He cocked his head, his ugly little gorilla nose twitching as though inviting Philip to share the treasure he had found.

Philip was cold. His socks and shoes squelched with each step. He jerked the lead sternly. 'Come on. Hurry up before the rain starts.'

Denise's house looked deserted, but he could hear her unlatching locks and security fittings in answer to his knock. Relief crossed her face as she saw Teddy. 'Oh, thank goodness. You've found him!' Her gaze moved to Philip's soaked clothing. 'Whatever happened to you?'

'Were you looking for him? I'm so sorry. I foolishly took him for a walk and we had a rather eventful outing.'

'I saw your car and wandered down to have a word. But you weren't there, and neither was Teddy. I did hope he'd gone with you.'

Philip explained the ordeal, though he played down the panic he'd experienced when it seemed he'd lost the dog. Denise listened and nodded. 'Len used to take him out fishing. You must have had a scare.'

'I thought he'd drowned. I'm about to go home, Mrs. Courtney. Will he be all right if I leave him at the cottage?'

'Leave him with me. I'll see he's dry and warm before he goes home. He won't stay the night. I've tried before. But he went with you quite willingly?'

Philip shrugged. He wasn't going to share his crazy thought that Teddy knew he was connected to Len. The idea was pure fantasy. He operated on logic, not canine psychic nonsense.

Denise's mind had no such qualms

as her gaze brightened with insight. 'I find that extraordinary, Philip. I know Teddy. He's a one-man dog. I've given up hoping he'll ever attach to anyone else. But he's recognized something you and your father share. Some physical imprint, or a mark of the spirit, like an aura . . .'

But Philip had no interest in auras and cut the conversation short. 'I'd better get going,' he said. 'We're in for a real downpour.' So far the rain had held off, but the lightning continued to play against the greenish sky.

'I hope it clears by midnight,' said Denise. 'Are you staying up to see the lunar eclipse?'

'I saw mention of it on the news. But no, I expect to be tucked up warmly in my bed.'

'They're rare, you know. And this one is a blood moon. They say it marks an eventful time for people.'

Denise obviously had nothing better to do than stand and chat, but the heat of Philip's recent panic had cooled, and he felt very cold in his wet clothing.

'You're sure you won't come in for a cup of tea?'

'Thanks, but no. I need to go home and change. But I hope the rain won't spoil your vigil. I'll say goodbye.'

As Philip turned to leave, Teddy ran to his feet and began pawing at his wet shoes. Ignoring his crazy impulse to scoop up the little dog and take it home with him, he made sure Denise had a good grip on Teddy's leash before he squelched back to his car. He had enough going on in his life without adding a needy pet to the list.

★　★　★

Carrying a large black umbrella, Denise Courtney walked down to the cottage to check on Teddy. She yawned, feeling sleep-deprived after waiting up to view the eclipse. Last night, standing at her window, she'd watched shredded clouds race across the distant globe as its silvery image gradually darkened. Blood moon, they called it. She wondered if the phenomenon affected the earth, and if animals could sense it. Something had set Teddy off. She'd heard him howling down there on Len's veranda.

She'd made cocoa and returned to the window, hugging her worn dressing gown around her thin frame. The murky color of the rufous moon was something to do with the refraction of the sun's rays . . . the sort of thing Len would have explained to her, lining up his matchboxes or pepper and salt shakers to demonstrate. She hated seeing his cottage engulfed in darkness. Death had come so quietly. Had Len been prepared? He wasn't the type of man to discuss his feelings.

She'd no-one to talk to about Len now. Nobody would understand why she felt bereaved. Yes, years ago she'd carried a torch for him, until she'd made her feelings plain and saw how she'd embarrassed him. The look on his face had made her feel like a flasher, bursting into his house in her birthday suit. Pretty quickly she'd set aside any romantic ideas. But, in time, they did find a mutual togetherness, living separately but walking their dogs, sharing their garden produce, solving the monster crossword in the weekend newspaper. They'd spent as much time together as many married couples did today. They'd bartered runner beans for strawberries, fresh eggs for tomato pickle. In those days it was the woman who cooked and sewed, the man who fixed fuses and tuned in the TV channels.

Sometimes Len would go quiet, withdrawn. Then she'd know there was a guest at the cottage. She minded her own business. Even then, she knew he was there. Yes, it was Len's presence that she missed so much. Loneliness frightened her now. She was ageing. Her family was scattered and her friends had moved on or passed away. Len's death had disturbed her sense of security, and she thought more about her own death. A time for change was upon her.

'Oh, Len! Fancy going off and

leaving me.' Oh lord, she was talking out loud. Going silly! She pushed open the gate and Teddy gave a welcome bark from the porch. 'There you are!' She carried a tidbit — a cooked sausage his keen nose scented at once. Greedily he snatched it from her fingers and ran to his hiding place under the steps.

The cottage was deserted again. She kept silent track of the work in progress. By the time they were done, the place would be a picture. Did Philip intend to sell? She was still bamboozled by the news that he was Len's son. Len had never once told her he'd had a child. Had he been married and realized too late that he'd made a ghastly mistake? The son had even less charm than his father. Touchy, almost rude, had been her first impression. If he didn't watch it, he'd lose that girl. Could it have happened already? She hadn't seen a sign of the yellow Volkswagen all week. If they'd broken up, she sensed how devastated he would be. Natalie might be young, perhaps flighty, but her nature was warm and spontaneous. Philip could certainly do with those traits to balance his cool nature. His reserve and guarded manner reminded her of Len. Len had painted, while Philip used his gifted hands in a kind of artistry on the human body. He must be at the top of his field to have separated those twin babies. But he wasn't a man you could flatter, any more than Len had wanted praise. It was as though they could never be satisfied; never feel they were good enough.

Funny how she'd felt free to offer Philip advice. In a different world, as she'd remarked to him, she could have married Len. Then Philip would have been her stepson. What a turn-up that would have been! But she'd got over her disappointment. Unrequited love was unprofitable. She and Len had found another kind of friendship — whereas that poor man had never even met his father.

She'd promised to dig out some photos for him. Perhaps she could do that later. Again the sky was overcast, subduing the lake's surface to the color of pewter. More heavy rain was forecast. The painters must have decided not to work, and again there was no sign of Natalie's cheery yellow VW.

Denise tried to coax Teddy from under the steps, but he stayed put, his eyes spying on her through the gap between the treads. She sighed. The poor little fellow must be disoriented, seeing the demolition going on around him. Why wouldn't he give up his vigil and move in with her? Stout-hearted and loyal he might be, but dogs were social pack animals. He needed warmth and company, just as she did.

'Teddy, one of these days we're going to have to accept that Len's not coming back.' She checked his food and water bowls and turned for home. Big drops were splashing on the excavations. They'd be a mud bath when the rain came down. Sighing, she raised her umbrella and trudged back to her empty house.

8

Natalie could still remember being taken to her father's bedside as he lay screened off by curtains in a public ward. He'd looked so weary, with barely the strength to pat her tiny hand. Young as she'd been, she'd known something dark and sinister had happened in this place. Her father had never come home. What had they done with him? Her mother cried often. Nobody told her why. Later, she'd learned the details of her father's illness, but the memories were ingrained. Natalie had never set foot in another hospital.

If Philip really knew the depths of her dread, he would reassure her, of course. The hospital was his second home. How could he possibly know how those clinical smells and sounds affected her? She was facing her greatest fear, and although Philip was kind and considerate, she needed something more from him. He was methodical and calm as he drove her to her appointments at the hospital. At home he took over the domestic chores, carefully folding clean laundry or concocting a shopping list with the same planning he no doubt brought to his job. But something was missing. He was the same man — reserved, self-contained. She hadn't set out to change him. They'd forged a workable routine together . . . friends with benefits, as the saying went.

No, it was Natalie who'd changed. Her diagnosis had stripped her of her power. Until now, she could always initiate sex to prove to herself she was desirable. Now the reflection that gazed back at her as she did her hair and applied her makeup was apprehensive. How would she look after her hair had been shorn and her brain had been tampered with? Would Philip still want her?

Already he was treating her differently. He'd made no attempt to raise the birth control issue. She'd expected he would have suggested condoms to tide them over, but sex seemed to have disappeared from their relationship. She was left with an anxious feeling of need. Her illusions had been shattered; she could no longer believe she was independent and simply enjoying a casual relationship with Philip.

Even before this crisis, she'd been questioning herself. Philip was so different from other men she'd known. If they were to break up, would she be able to walk away as easily as she'd done in the past? He meant well, but the closeness she needed wasn't to be found in his efforts at housework or cooking. She was driven to raise touchy issues, like the subject of his father. Philip had been emotional ever since he'd received the lawyer's news of his inheritance, but as usual he hid his feelings of rejection behind a sarcastic barrier. If she passed on Denise's confidence that Len had been gay, surely he would have to see the awful dilemma his father had faced, and the reason why his mother felt abandoned. Perhaps the police had been involved. No wonder he had walked away.

But Philip just shrugged when she shared Denise's story. 'Yes, she told me. She seems to be very free with personal information.' He sounded thoroughly dismissing.

'She wasn't just gossiping, Philip. She loved him. Don't you think it's sad?'

'I couldn't care less what went on between her and my father.'

'Why didn't you talk to me when you found out?'

'It didn't occur to me. Why on earth would you be interested?'

'Because it makes sense of why he left you. What concerns you concerns me, doesn't it? Isn't that what a relationship is supposed to be?'

'I'm sorry, Natalie. I really can't answer that.'

Normally she would have let him walk away, shutting down as he usually did when he was disturbed. But her anger exploded. Here she was, sharing the deepest crisis of her life with him, and he was still trying to shut her out of his own private life. 'Then think about it! Are you going to sulk about your father for the rest of your life? You have the explanation now of why he left, and you won't see it. I think it says a lot about your mother, too. She probably wouldn't let him near you. I see your father as a victim. But you go on brooding and storing up your resentment. Just as you do with your mother.'

'Is there anyone else in my family you want to discuss?' His face was white, his lips compressed. He was completely still, as though controlling immense anger. She knew she was pushing him over the brink. She left him, running up the stairs in tears.

* * *

Philip was still mulling over Natalie's outburst as he chopped vegetables for the stir-fry he planned to make for dinner. Why had she interfered in his private affairs? He couldn't deal with displays of emotion. Anger transported him back to his own helpless childhood, and the ugly words and drunken assaults he could hear through his flimsy bedroom wall. Sadness confronted him with the image of his mother, her back turned to him in one of her depressive interludes.

He'd developed strategies to cope. He wasn't a pugnacious type of man. So he escaped, avoiding the triggers that charged his whole body like a blaring alarm system, alerting his nerves and knotting his gut. He held himself together and shut down, dismissing those alarm sirens to a secret repository he kept locked in his heart. As a result, at work or in his romantic life, plenty of people implied he was unfeeling. He knew his bedside manner was lacking, and his plain speaking was interpreted as rudeness. But he did not see this as anybody's business but his own.

As for the women in his past who had presumed to delve and probe, eventually he'd sent them packing. What did they expect of him? Surely a man should be judged by his actions? He didn't want to share his feelings, or talk about them; in fact, he didn't want to have any feelings. People ruled by their feelings destroyed lives; broke marriages and hearts. Look at the mess Len McLeod had made of his own and several others' lives! His father had suddenly invaded his life, opened Pandora's box, and conveniently left Philip to deal with the results. Now he'd upset Natalie; the last thing she needed at the moment.

He found the non-stick spray and coated the pan, setting it to heat on the element. He and Natalie had a perfectly good living arrangement, accommodating her occasional tantrum or his involvement with work. She could be entrancing when she turned on her feminine wiles. She was lovely, smart and ambitious. The age difference did not seem to pose any problems. At times she asked his advice or came to sit on his knee, seeming to allot him a paternal role. He'd even wondered whether they might move toward something more permanent. He was trying now to show his support. What else did she want? He would have to make a bigger effort, that was all.

Tipping the diced chicken into the pan, he stood stirring the sizzling chunks, lost in strategies. He could take over the repairs at the cottage altogether, and push to hasten the date of her proposed surgery. He tried to think of other concessions. A short holiday? She had some bee in her bonnet about meeting his mother. Very well, that could be easily arranged. Perhaps if she met Irene face to face, she would understand why Philip found the relationship so difficult. Since Len had made himself a presence in their lives again, every conversation with Irene felt potentially explosive. He'd never managed to outgrow his discomfort with her highly-strung, unpredictable nature. Now he dreaded visiting her. He had to force himself to go, the knot in his gut tightening with each step he climbed toward her pitiful little life. Her poverty reached out to him, seeping past his rational mind, reminding him she'd lived a life of sacrifice to raise him to where he was today — a successful surgeon. She refused the one way he felt he could repay her, turning down his offers of material help. He grew stiff when she embraced him, and turned his cheek away from her needy kiss. Yes, she wanted something else from him, but what? In fact she was like Natalie, who now wanted something mysterious enough to send her running up the stairs away from him, in tears. What on earth did women want?

Exasperated, he shoveled the vegetables into the pan, stirred the mixture and checked that the rice hadn't boiled dry. Turning off the heat, he went upstairs to tell Natalie the food was ready. After dinner, they were going to sit down and thrash out what exactly it was that would make Natalie happy. For the life of him, he couldn't understand her.

To Philip's great relief, the evening ended better than it had begun. Neither he nor Natalie referred to their argument. They finished the meal, then settled together on the couch, and she rested her head on his shoulder. Philip breathed in the fragrance of her perfume, allowing his fingers to glide through the soft length of her thick, dark hair. While he stroked her she stayed silent and passive.

'Will they shave my head?' She suddenly opened her eyes, turning her gaze to meet his, and he realized her thoughts had been elsewhere.

'Yes, where they operate.' He was carefully avoiding any reference to the details of the procedure. Natalie wouldn't be awake then. There was no need to alarm her. He sensed she had dropped the subject of his father, and decided on his olive branch. 'I thought we'd visit my mother at her unit tomorrow, after you have the MRI.' He knew she wasn't looking forward to the scan, but it was

218

the last procedure she had to have before the surgery.

Natalie sat up. 'Do you want me to come?' She sounded surprised.

'It's an old custom, I believe. Meeting the parent.'

'Only when you're courting.' She smiled up at him.

'It will do Mum good. And it's time I introduced her to my girlfriend.'

'Sure I'm still your girlfriend?'

'Absolutely. As long as you have no objection.'

'You're sure you want damaged goods?'

'Natalie! Don't say that!' Bending over her, he dropped gentle kisses on her head.

'I won't break, Philip.'

She tried to tempt him, angling her mouth against his lips, but he resisted his predictable response. Making love would set her pulse racing. It wasn't right to excite her, despite his surge of desire. He didn't want to remind her that her AVM was behaving unpredictably. Who knew what stimulation might trigger the treacherous little knot of vessels to burst?

He disentangled himself and stood up, gathering the plates and cutlery. She followed him to the kitchen. 'I feel so bad, leaving the cottage half-finished, and you neglecting your work because of me.'

He set down the dishes and hugged her tight. 'Everything will be all right.' She leaned into him, seeming to believe his words.

* * *

The visit to Irene went surprisingly well. Philip had painted his mother in such unflattering terms that Natalie expected to meet a neurotic, bitter shell of a woman. Instead, Irene presented as an attractive and interesting person. Her face retained a striking bone structure that must have been a factor in her early modeling role with Len. Her youthful figure, despite the drab clothes, moved with a grace unexpected in a woman of her age. She was clearly devoted to her only son.

Natalie watched, feeling sorry for the woman's efforts to draw Philip out, while he brushed aside her queries and shared none of his problems. She could understand that his father might be a touchy subject to raise; but if he always treated Irene like this, it was no wonder his relationship with her was stagnant. In his mother's presence he seemed stripped of his normal authority, as though he was still a little boy. Well, Natalie wasn't so different with her own mother, on the rare occasions they spoke on the phone. Surely there should come a point where parent and child could move past their early roles and relate simply as adults? Had he even mentioned that Natalie was living with him?

Irene made discreet inquiries as she poured tea into three cups and set out a plate of homemade biscuits. 'You're a nurse at the hospital?'

'That's the last job I'd want!' She saw Irene's surprise. 'I'm an interior designer.'

'Oh. I thought Philip said you were both coming here from the hospital?'

She seemed an easy person to confide in. Natalie explained she had to have surgery, adding that she was very nervous about the operation. Irene reached over and quietly took her hand. The kindly gesture touched Natalie. She'd been feeling a childish need for maternal support, and several times had been on the point of phoning her own mother in Brisbane. But their conversations were strained and infrequent. Jackie Norris always showed interest in Natalie's life, but as usual the house would be full of recovering wildlife that required her care. Asking her to drop everything and rush to Natalie's side was just not practical. Whenever her mother tried to explain her predicament, Natalie felt herself revert to a resentful child, faced with the fact that Jackie couldn't put her first. Turning to her mother was as big a hurdle for Natalie as Philip's attitude to Irene.

Irene had no such inhibitions in

sharing her evident pride in her son. She described Philip in his youth, quiet and studious, poring over his homework, learning how to play chess from a library book, and taking part in concerts at the migrant hall in town. She fetched a photograph album and flipped the pages, pushing the book across the table to Natalie.

'Philip used to dance?' Natalie smiled at the image of several little boys dressed up in baggy Cossack pants and boots.

'He was very good, squatting and kicking out his legs like an expert.'

'You never told me, Philip!'

'I'd forgotten,' he muttered.

'I've got to see this! Can you still do it?'

'I doubt it.' He stood up. 'We should go. Do you need anything, Mother?' By 'anything', he obviously meant money.

There was a shift in Irene's expression — a shade of disappointment, as though her son saw her as nothing but a burden. 'No, thank you,' was all she said.

An awkward silence hung between mother and son. Natalie felt she was being rushed. She would have liked to stay and chat; to ask Irene about her background, how she came to Australia, what interested her now. 'I see you have a budgie.' She walked over to the large cage, noting it was immaculately clean. The little bird considered her inquiringly. As a rule, Natalie disliked the idea of caging birds. Her mother's principle that a creature should be returned to its natural habitat had been instilled into her. But pet birds like this were bred in captivity and would not survive for a day in the wild.

'I'd like a cat or dog.' Irene had followed her and was making affectionate clicks with her tongue as the bird responded. 'But the regulations here don't allow it.'

'I know what you mean. I grew up in a home full of animals and birds. My mother works for the wildlife rescue service.'

'She must be a very kind person.'

'I suppose she is.' The thought surprised Natalie, who perceived her mother as eccentric.

Philip had walked out to the steps and was standing there, his posture aloof, as though he couldn't wait to be on his way.

Natalie turned back to Irene. 'I've enjoyed meeting you.'

The older woman pressed a kiss on Natalie's cheek. 'I wish you well with your operation. I hope to see you both soon.' The poor woman obviously longed for a warmer relationship with her son. His distant manner must be hurtful.

'Thank you, Irene. Once I'm back on my feet, will you come round for a meal?'

'I'd like that very much.' She stood on her balcony, waving as they reached the car park.

Natalie fastened her seat belt as Philip started the engine. 'I liked your mother. She's warm and friendly. Nothing like the neurotic sort of person you described.'

'Is that a fact?' Philip sounded

disbelieving and drove home in silence.

Strange, how two people could perceive a situation in radically different ways. But Natalie didn't need to have another confrontation with him. A couple of things Irene had said suggested that Natalie had some bridges to mend with her own mother. And before going under the surgeon's knife was probably the right time to attend to that.

★ ★ ★

On the morning of Natalie's admission, Philip had thought she was going to back out altogether. It had taken all his persuasion to drive her to the hospital and get her into the lift to ride up to her allocated ward. Now, as he ate a couple of very average ham-and-mustard sandwiches at the hospital caféteria, the day's events replayed in his mind.

Natalie's reluctance over her surgery was far more than the normal apprehension anyone might feel. She was genuinely phobic, finally confiding in him how her father's death in hospital had affected her. He'd felt terribly sorry for her. His reassurances simply drifted past her without registering. She'd had a hunted look, imploring him to stay while the nurse wheeled in her prep trolley to record BP and temperature and fill out admission forms. When she handed Natalie her theatre gown, he slipped away — carrying his last impression of Natalie's terrified gaze as the anesthetist came in to interview her. These were the pragmatic aspects of surgery that he rarely associated with the unconscious patients who lay ready on the operating table for his skilled knife.

He wondered why he felt so upset. The body took a while to recover from any invasion, but without intervention the outcome would be much worse. People just had to put up with the inconveniences. But somehow all he could feel was Natalie's fear. Surgery could go wrong. Sometimes the body was a ticking time bomb, concealing secrets that could make a surgeon wish he had any other profession than that of healer. What if he lost Natalie?

He reproached his mind for producing useless thoughts and pushed away the crusts of his food. Surely she must be out of theater by now? She'd been first on the afternoon list. He'd checked at four p.m. but there'd been no news.

The weak spring sunshine bathing the outdoor courtyard was fading. The serrated fingers of ferns and palms traced the courtyard floor with moving shadows as a breeze stirred the foliage. He gazed at the sculpture — a view usually too familiar to hold his attention. Today the figures trapped in their compassionate pose reached his awareness. They seemed to be holding each other, exchanging strength and comfort, as though facing or surviving some traumatic event.

He felt anything but strong as he made his way up to the recovery ward. His heart sank as he entered and checked the occupied beds. Natalie was still not back from surgery. What was taking so long? His stomach clenched. It wasn't his place to push his way into theater and see for himself what was going on. He'd expected the procedure to take about two hours, but here it was dusk outside, though in the brightly lit hospital corridors it was hard to distinguish night from day. He lingered at the window, gazing down the long shaft to the courtyard below, where architects had tried to balance the essentially mechanical aspects of a hospital's function. He thought of Natalie, intubated and sustained by drugs while the private world of her brain yielded up its secrets.

He heard the ward telephone ring. A nurse came to speak to him. 'She's on her way from theater now, Doctor.'

He knew what to expect, but stood aside, feeling helpless, when the still figure was wheeled to a waiting bed and transferred by the orderly and nurse. He could see the white bandage swathing Natalie's skull. Efficiently, the nurse began checking and writing down recordings on a chart.

She nodded to Philip. 'Do you want to sit with her?'

He took the indicated chair. How often he'd walked into this unit in his blue scrubs, detached as he checked a patient or wrote up a medication regime. Natalie's face was pale against the white hospital linen and her eyes were closed. As he gently traced the dark wing of an eyebrow, he was struck by the randomness of life. A surgeon accepted the capricious nature of illnesses and accidents, and did what he was trained to do. He realized it was much harder simply to sit and wait for consciousness to return, hoping a loved one had been healed. He stayed there, keeping watch, while Natalie lay immobile and unreachable.

* * *

Natalie's first post-operative days were shocking. She had never known real pain, and losing control over her life frightened her. Doctors and nurses continually interrupted her days, and even sleep brought no sense of rest. The claustrophobia she'd experienced in the MRI machine returned to haunt her. Imagining the disfigured scalp under her dressings started tears whenever she touched the bandages. She had an urge to jump out of bed and escape the terrible feeling that she'd emerged from the operation damaged in some way.

Her plan had been to regain her independence as soon as she could. But the first time she was helped out of bed, her legs gave way, and only the nurses' support saved her from crumpling to the floor. She required days of physio before she could walk at all, hanging on to a walking frame. She remembered seeing frail old people pushing them along, their shopping baskets dangling from a hook. There was one terrible day when the bandages were removed, uncovering twenty-four staples in her scalp. The drugs they gave her for her throbbing headaches made her lethargic and irritable, and she wished people would go away and leave her alone. At the same time, she had to accept help, in a humiliating way she'd never known even as a child.

After ten days she was allowed to go home under Philip's care. He pushed her in a wheelchair from the ward, as hospital regulations required. The ride home was a nightmare. She groaned and snapped at Philip, as every bump and jerk felt magnified until she thought she was on some fiendish fun-fair ride. The stairs in the apartment were a problem. Philip had bought a portable bed and set it up downstairs. He'd extended his leave to help her adjust to the limitations of her newly frail body.

'What's wrong with me? I feel so tired.' Even reading a magazine felt beyond her.

'It's perfectly normal, sweetheart. Your brain's had a shake-up, that's all.'

She could hear him pottering in the kitchen, making one of the specialties he'd recently added to the pre-packed dinners from the frozen section of the supermarket. When Philip cooked, he laid out his utensils with surgical precision, and presented his meals with the aplomb of a waiter.

He did not hide his look of disappointment when she pushed away his offerings after a few mouthfuls. 'Was there something wrong? Too much seasoning?'

'No. I'm not hungry.'

He helped her to the downstairs en suite, stood by while she showered, and plumped up her pillows like a well-trained nurse. And she wondered when she would ever feel like a healthy young woman again. Surely Philip would tire of this weary invalid inhabiting her body? The flickers of anxiety flared, then grew dull and died, as though nothing mattered. The glaring Australian sun warned of approaching summer, but her own world had shrunk to this room, with the air-conditioner humming and the curtains drawn.

Only when Philip returned from a

shopping trip, sweating and hot, did she remember the busy world beyond the apartment. She wasn't supposed to drive for several months. Philip was trying to get her motivated, suggesting brief outings. She thought he had no idea of the leaden effort it was just to get dressed and walk out to the kitchen. He tried to involve her with talk of the cottage. 'I've arranged for an art appraiser to go through my father's paintings. Would you like to come?'

Natalie shook her head. His look of disappointment did not move her.

'It's time you moved back upstairs,' he suggested a few days later.

She thought of climbing the stairs. 'I'm not ready.'

'Natalie, you need to make an effort.'

She felt criticized and tears rose in her eyes. She blinked them away. He was probably right. The doctors had told her the operation was a success. Was Philip perhaps more concerned over her slow recovery than he'd shown? For both their sakes she must get back to normal.

He had returned to work, becoming lost again in his life at the hospital. When she inquired about the separated twins, he just said they'd been discharged, and she did not detect any of the anxious concern he'd shown for them while they were under his care. Perhaps he had lost interest in her own crisis?

She practiced climbing the stairs and found she could make it to the top. 'I think I'll move back upstairs.'

He smiled, pleased with her. Had he been missing her in the bed beside him? 'That's the first decision you've made since you came home,' was all he said, and she thought his words seemed clinical. Apart from mentioning the art appraiser, he never referred to the cottage. What had happened to her project? She seemed to recall Josh phoning her once, just after she'd come home; but if they'd had a conversation, she couldn't remember what was said.

It was time to snap out of this lethargy. Thinking back to Teddy and the days she'd spent with Josh, working side by side as easy companions, a pang of nostalgia shot through her. She remembered his kindness. Somehow he'd always been on hand to help, without any suggestion he was doing her a favor. She waited until Philip was at work, then dressed and searched her handbag for Josh's business card. She would ring him, let him know she was over her convalescence, and find out if the repairs and painting were complete. But his mobile rang unanswered and, already losing her drive, she postponed her decision.

Natalie stretched out on the downstairs couch, thinking if she could drive she could have hopped in her car and taken a run over to the cottage to see what was happening there. She needed to get over her dependence on Philip. He'd been so caring, but they needed to build a new relationship together. He'd turned to her one night, his touches too gentle and tentative, as though she might break. She hadn't known how to respond.

When Josh returned her call, her spirits lifted. He could always cheer her up, and he seemed pleased to hear from her. 'You sound good, Nat. I rang a while back, but your partner said you weren't taking phone calls.'

'No. I was a bit out of it for a while. Scrambled brain.'

Josh just laughed. Well, how could he possibly know what she'd been through? 'You sound fine now. When are you coming over to see our progress? Philip pulled us off the job for a while, but we're just finishing the last of the carpentry and painting. The place is crying out for your ideas.'

'I'll be coming soon.'

'Good. I've missed you.' His tone was affectionate. After she switched off, she wondered why she'd repressed her impulse to reciprocate his words. Somehow her natural inclination to flirt felt wrong now — and she didn't know her new identity well enough to take any chances.

9

As Philip parked outside the cottage, he hoped the art appraiser would be punctual. Work at the hospital had built up during his absence. He'd returned to find his theater and consulting lists were packed, and on top of that, the hospital was preparing to take part in a policy conference to clarify procedures relating to the dreaded Ebola epidemic presently raging in west Africa. Several of the medical staff would be chosen to fly north to Darwin, to study treatment regimes and protocols in the event that a full-blown epidemic happened to reach Australia's shores.

He had discussed the option with his colleague, Bryan Mason. 'I wouldn't want to go,' the surgeon admitted. 'I can't imagine working with such a fatal epidemic. Surgery's clean! You have some past experience in tropical medicine, I recall.'

'Yes, in the Pacific,' Philip said. 'One can imagine the devastation if Ebola happened to bypass all the security precautions. I just feel it's wise to be prepared.'

Bryan smiled and gave him a friendly pat on the shoulder. 'Not for me. I'm not a hero. But why not apply, if it interests you? You can always say no if you change your mind.'

'I'll think about it. I'm fairly committed with Natalie. Her convalescence is moving slower than I expected.'

'Everyone's different. She strikes me as an anxious young woman. You might need to encourage her to make an effort.'

Philip's spirits sank when Bryan confirmed his own impression. His medical mind was puzzled. Physically, he thought Natalie was well enough to resume her former activities. It was as though she'd lost all her motivation. Without knowing her phobia about sickness and hospitals, it was possible that Bryan had hit on the psychological reason for her slow recovery. Philip's own medical association as a doctor wouldn't be helping. She probably needed young people, a cheerful environment, perhaps a man her own age. He'd done his best, but was he holding her back?

Now he checked his watch. He had an appointment with administration back at the hospital in a couple of hours. His chest felt tight. He should be used to this feeling of pressure. Ever since this cottage had cursed his life, he hadn't had a day's relaxation. Natalie seemed to think he should be grateful for his father's gift, but it had come with too many strings attached, dragging up all the hurts of his childhood.

As he wandered across the newly laid turf and pavers to open up the cottage, Teddy appeared from round the corner. Philip stooped to give him a pat. Since the upsetting episode when the dog had come close to drowning, Philip often found himself thinking of the animal. He'd dreamed of the dog in dangerous situations, running headlong into busy traffic or tumbling down a deep well, while Philip made risky attempts to rescue him. Teddy was unwanted — a symbol, perhaps, of his own childhood memories.

Reminding himself he had enough on his plate without fretting over a dog, he walked into the cottage. No doubt about it — Josh and his father had done a good job since resuming work. Additional windows added light and spaciousness to the rooms. Only the studio retained its air of clutter and homemade modifications. He picked up a folder that had been left on the kitchen table and scanned the note. It was signed by Denise Courtney and pinned to the cover. *Philip, your father left these drawings in my care. I think they are meant for you.*

Inside were several charcoal sketches. As Philip carefully separated them from the interleaved tissue paper, his heart beat faster. He knew he was seeing an example of his father's artistic talent in these stirring depictions. They conveyed simple themes: a woman standing in a model's pose; the same woman, cradling a baby; a chuckling six-month-old boy, waving a toy rabbit; and on the margin of the papers, a man excluded, his expression twisted with grief as he turned his back on his family. A final drawing was titled 'Self Portrait'. The lines were jagged and ugly, depicting a haggard man, his hands bound together at the wrists and his head drooping in an attitude of shame.

In a sense the images were conventional, and quite unlike the artist's developed style. Yet the marks scratched so long ago with a simple piece of willow charcoal were deeply moving. They expressed such a sense of loss that they brought tears to Philip's eyes. It was as though his father stood in front of him, expressing now the words of love and regret that Philip had never heard. But his body vibrated with cold shivers as he rejected that sense of a presence. *Too late, Len!* He closed the folder, feeling an angry urge to destroy the sketches.

A volley of barks, followed by the art appraiser's knock, saved him from his destructive impulse. She introduced herself as Mary-Lou Barnes, and said she worked for the art gallery. Her attitude was professional as she carried out her methodical inspection of the studio works, photographing and listing the canvases one by one. While she said they were interesting, her comments suggested these minor works were only of secondary interest, as examples of an artist's unrealized experimental work. Philip gathered there was nothing of much financial value. Not that he cared. As far as he was concerned, she could take the lot and burn them. His only plan had been to give any proceeds to his mother.

With that thought, he fetched the folder of sketches that Denise had left for him. As she leafed through the pages, the woman's manner changed to one of avid interest. The images were unsigned and carried no date, but she seemed confident they slotted in among a few similar works from a stagnant period in the late seventies when she said little was known of Len's life. 'How interesting they have surfaced now!' The woman seemed excited by her find.

Philip shrugged. 'Take them with you, if you like.'

'But these should be in a safe until they're valued.' She sounded shocked.

'Well, I don't want them. What do you suggest?'

'Don't be too hasty. You might be surprised at their value, and the gallery might be interested in acquiring them.' She paused, looking around at the renovations. 'On that note, do you plan to sell McLeod's cottage? You've done a thorough job in restoring the place. Have you thought of approaching the local council?'

'Why would I do that?' He was aware he was running late for his appointment, but the woman was suggesting possibilities he'd never considered.

'Historic value. Len McLeod's already a significant figure in the art world. His work's only going to appreciate. I'm guessing his home would be of interest to art lovers, tourists and the local community.' She was visibly impressed by his father's standing. This woman had no idea of the mayhem stirred up by Philip's absent father. In her eyes he was a great artist, first and foremost. His personal faults did not matter.

Philip's anger had ebbed. It seemed pointless, somehow. His father had been gifted, and flawed, like all humans. Who could judge him? He was gone, and had left his work as his silent testimony.

Rain had set in again when he saw Mary-Lou off the premises and went back to collect the drawings and lock up. Teddy, familiar with departures, emerged from under the veranda and dogged Philip's heels as he fastened his rain jacket and headed to his car. 'Not you again!' The dripping dog barked and shook vigorously, scattering water like a halo. Cocking his head, he appeared to be waiting for an invitation to go to the beach for another fun outing. Philip paused. It seemed so heartless simply to drive off and leave the little fellow on his own.

He heard a call and saw Denise Courtney making her way down the slope, waving her bulky golf umbrella to attract his attention. He hadn't time to chat, but she seemed determined to speak to him.

'Philip! Did you find the drawings I left for you?'

'Yes, thank you.' He did not expand on the art appraiser's evaluation.

'I dropped them off when the painters were here.'

'I see.' He'd been wondering whether she had a key. Pulling out his own central locking device, he fiddled with it, hoping Denise would read his body language. She was hurrying; foolishly, he thought, on such slippery ground. At her age, a false step could be enough to send her to hospital with a fracture.

Instinctively he held up his hand, telling her to slow down. His appointment would simply have to be rearranged.

'It must be fate!' She laughed, disregarding his unwelcoming scowl. 'I've been wondering what on earth to do about the dog.' She went on to explain that she had to go to Melbourne to a funeral for her sister's husband. 'The family will be so offended if I don't attend. They expect me to stay for a week. They've even booked my flight. I have to go first thing in the morning. Could you possibly take Teddy?'

Philip stood in the rain, considering just for a moment. For he already knew the answer to her problem. As the owner of the property, he wondered why it had taken him so long to deal with Teddy. Skulking and hiding was no life for a homeless dog. He had to be surrendered, if he was ever to find himself a new home. But Denise would cancel her flight rather than agree.

'I'll take him with me.' No need to go into details.

Denise's cornflower-blue eyes sparked with relief. 'Thank goodness! He'll be a lamb. You have a garden?'

'I have a large apartment.' She didn't need to know he lived on the second floor of an elite complex where pet ownership was fraught with rules and regulations. Today was a write-off anyway. He'd take Teddy to the pound. He brushed aside Denise's gratitude. Although she would resent his decision, it was the only responsible thing to do.

He loaded Teddy in the car, gathered his leash and feeding bowls, and waved to Denise. Once he was out of her sight, he pulled up, ignoring his sense of guilt as he checked his local directory. He'd had to make many hard decisions during his working life. Decided, he programmed his route into his GPS and headed straight to the pound.

The building was located away from built-up areas. He could see why. A cacophony of barks and howls greeted him as he pulled up outside the reception sign. Teddy clambered onto the back seat and peered through the glass, adding his own voice to the din. Philip checked that the leash was firmly clipped before allowing him outside, and Teddy tugged him toward the door, scampering to investigate the myriad smells his sensitive nose had discerned. The racket inside the shed echoed off the corrugated iron walls.

The desk was deserted. Philip opened a door and found it led through to the kennel area, where an array of caged dogs of various breeds and sizes expressed their response to a visitor. Different as they were, their message seemed full of hope as most of them dashed forward to the wire to investigate. A few depressed-looking creatures stayed huddled at the backs of their enclosures. En masse, their plight cut through Philip's defenses. Looking around at the sterile wire cages, cramped rectangles with cement floors and metal water bowls, Philip turned and hastily retreated with Teddy.

An attendant had taken his seat behind the desk. He barely glanced at

Teddy as he pushed a piece of paper across the desk. 'You want to surrender the dog? Fill out this form please. Note any defects or bad habits. Are the vaccinations up to date?'

'He's not really mine . . .' Philip began, and the man eyed him suspiciously. 'I inherited him. The owner died.' It was obvious that Teddy's history was of little interest to the attendant, who had probably hardened himself after years of receiving abandoned animals. 'How long will it take to find him a suitable home?' Philip persisted. His uncomfortable feeling intensified as Teddy lay down, his globular eyes gazing up with patient trust.

'Depends. Luck of the draw. It's a busy time of year.' Unsmiling, the man considered Teddy. 'He's not a puppy, and he's no pedigree. We'll have a shot at placing him somewhere. Maybe keep him for a month.'

Philip was far from satisfied. 'And then what? Euthanize him?'

'We do our best. There's only limited

space here.' He waved toward the closed door. 'It's simple arithmetic.'

Behind the closed entrance to the kennels, a fresh volley of barking suggested the pent-up frustration of creatures denied nature's normal patterns. Philip knew the world wasn't an ideal place. There were countries where human beings were living in conditions worse than these animals. He was reminded in an odd way of the hospital, where people became patients, confined to bed and stripped of the roles that made their lives worthwhile. But, 'simple arithmetic'? He couldn't live with himself if he deserted Teddy to take his chance in such an unpromising atmosphere. His heart made the decision, and he stepped back from the desk.

'Thanks for your time.' He reached for his wallet, and placed a couple of bills in the donation box. 'I'll try another option.'

The attendant thanked him and stepped out to give Teddy a farewell pat. 'No problem.'

Dumping Teddy on the back seat, Philip turned the car. It was too late now to take his passenger back to the cottage. Philip was officially a dog owner. But that didn't mean he was comfortable with the idea. As he drove home, his thoughts churned with the problems he now faced with the animal. He knew it was common enough these days for people to keep indoor pets. But how did they manage the needs for exercise, hygiene and toileting? How did you stop a dog from barking, if you were away at work? What if they were destructive? The small dog with his gorilla expression and protruding eyes came complete with responsibilities Philip had no idea how to fulfill. He could only hope Natalie would help him decide on solutions. She'd grown up in a house full of animals.

Teddy, however, was unperturbed by these issues. Delighted to be going for another ride, he struggled over the console and tried to sit on Philip's knee. Shoved onto the passenger seat, he set about making himself a comfortable nest, his sharp little claws digging at the upholstery as he circled and sank down with a contented grunt. This sort of activity must be why parents strapped their toddlers into car seats. You couldn't have a dog jumping around, distracting the driver.

Philip pulled up at a red light, parallel to a truck with an open tray where an aggressive cattle dog was secured by a short chain. Spotting Teddy, it barked ferociously, and appeared ready to leap at Philip's car. It was obvious to Philip that if he did, he would probably hang himself. Teddy responded with his own attack, his hackles raised as he scrabbled on the window, growling fiercely. Did he have no sense of scale? That cattle dog would devour him in a couple of bites.

The wait seemed interminable before the light turned green. Anxious to break up the escalating confrontation, Philip accelerated with a sharp jerk. As his tires squealed, Teddy fell off the seat, yelped with fright and urinated on the car mat. Philip groaned. Food. He had no dog food. Somehow he just couldn't face a trip to the store. He'd read it was illegal to leave a dog locked up in a vehicle. Surely he had something in the freezer?

He found himself speeding home-ward, his radar directing him to get to Natalie as fast as he could. She would know what to do. He'd followed a crazy impulse — an impulse, he now saw, that was completely impractical. He felt genu-inely sad as he glanced across at the dog, until he saw that Teddy, deciding to vacate his puddle, was clawing his way up the cream leather upholstery.

'Sorry, fella. This isn't working out.' He wrinkled his nose. He hadn't planned on shampooing the interior of his car today.

Back at his apartment block, he unloaded the dog, allowed him to sniff around the small garden beds that framed the entrance, and lugged the unwilling canine into the lift, preparing to offload him onto

Natalie while he took his car back to the nearest detailing station.

★　★　★

As usual, Natalie's day had dragged. She'd heard the same news items over and over — news that belonged to a remote world she no longer inhabited. Her mind relentlessly circled around the hospital, the surgery, and her struggle to present a normal façade. She doubted Philip was deceived. He was starting to drop diplomatic hints that she should try and resume normal life.

Nobody understood how deeply this cloud of inertia had sucked her into its fog. Except, surprisingly, Philip's mother. She'd telephoned to ask Natalie how she was, and they'd shared a personal conversation. Irene had been sympathetic, comparing Natalie's story with her own past battles with depression. Natalie had ended up inviting her for a visit. Whatever Philip's impression of his mother, Natalie liked her and was grateful for her understanding. But so far, she hadn't found a way to motivate herself. A repetitive voice mocked her with the idea that she was unneeded.

Today, having fallen asleep halfway through an old movie, she was awakened by a phone call from Josh. 'Hi, beautiful! I have a surprise to show you.' His ebullient tone made her wonder if she'd given him come-on signals in the past. Her memories of the cottage, Teddy, and Josh were all hazy. She'd always told herself that her flirting was just fun. But her self-confidence had deserted her and left her with the uncomfortable feeling that she'd been keeping her options open, never committing to one person. Philip had certainly proven himself, providing everything she'd needed during her health crisis. What had she done for him? The thought made her uncomfortable.

Ignoring his familiar greeting, Natalie tried to sound business-like. 'Why are you calling?'

'We've completed your partner's brief

on the cottage. Dad has one or two final suggestions. Plus, I really want to show you my surprise.'

Here was her motivation to go out. Instead, all she could do was to remind him her doctor had yet to lift his ban on her driving.

Josh brushed aside her excuse. 'I could give you a lift.'

How could she explain how weak she was? It took ages even to get dressed. He clearly had no idea how the operation had changed her life. Josh seemed to live in a different world from hers, and she wondered how she'd ever considered having a fling with him. To get rid of him, she agreed to do an inspection, promising to ring him in the next few days to arrange a time. She hung up with a sense of misgiving.

She was standing in front of the bathroom mirror, pensively considering the design of a turban to cover her short regrowth of hair, when she heard Philip shout her name. He sounded urgent, quite unlike himself, and she hurried downstairs, wondering if there was some emergency.

If Philip had walked through the door with an extra-terrestrial visitor, she could hardly have been more surprised. The problem at the doorway was Teddy, propped like a cartoon dog who'd skidded to a halt at the edge of a precipice. Clearly he perceived the apartment as a trap, and his hackles stood on end. Expressing his displeasure at the expansive surface, devoid of grass, earth, bone or treat, he was barking furiously as he glared up at Philip.

Natalie crossed the room and sank to her knees, trying to soothe the distressed animal. The arrival of Teddy and the helpless expression on Philip's face enabled her to take control. As Philip manhandled the dog over the threshold and slammed the door, she took the leash from his hand. 'Why have you brought him here? I thought dogs aren't allowed.'

Philip groaned. 'Don't remind me. I had a mental lapse. It's a long story.

Can you shut him up?'

'Probably.' In the kitchen, Natalie found a block of cheese and cut off a chunk, waving it enticingly as she called the dog. Diverted, Teddy at once obeyed and sat at her feet, his small nose twitching. Natalie gave him the treat. Since childhood she'd seen her mother prioritize the needs of newly rescued animals. Food was often high on the agenda. She felt a surge of unaccustomed energy as her mind flipped into gear. The dog was one issue; Philip was the other. Something extraordinary must have caused him to go against the building's rules and regulations, not to mention his own views. 'What happened, Philip?'

He sounded thoroughly confused when he spoke. 'I took him to the pound, but there was no assurance they'd find him a decent home.'

'What about Denise?'

'She's going to Melbourne for a funeral. I suppose I realized I'm the official owner of everything at the cottage. Including him.' He scowled at Teddy, who had enjoyed his snack and was now looking around for more.

Natalie eyed him. 'Sit!' Teddy sat. 'Lie down!' The dog instantly obeyed. 'He's been trained, obviously.' She rewarded him with another chunk of cheese.

'Is that suitable food for him?'

'Only as a treat. We'll have to get him some kibble at the store. Let's take him out. We can stop by a park and exercise him.'

'Too late. He already peed in my car.'

'Oh dear!' Natalie repressed a smile, knowing how Philip liked to keep his vehicle immaculate. 'If you drive, we can take my car, and pick up some upholstery shampoo as well.'

'You feel up to it?' He was looking at her in surprise. 'You haven't been out for weeks.'

'Have to start sometime. He needs exercise. We don't want another accident on the floor rug or the bed.'

'The bed?' Philip was looking at her in horror. 'I'm not sleeping with him.'

Natalie just smiled. Dogs had ingratiating ways that Philip couldn't begin to fathom. 'Of course not. I'll get the keys.'

'What about dinner?'

'We can pick up a take-out. Let's go!'

★　★　★

Within a few days, Teddy had settled in to his changed surroundings and accepted his new home. Philip's misgivings were fading. The dog did not show destructive leanings and quickly assumed his role as third member of the family. During the day, Natalie exercised him, benefiting herself from the fresh air. Philip took over the evening outings when she was tired.

He was relieved on several counts — Natalie had found a purpose, and he quite enjoyed the brisk walks with Teddy. There was a social aspect to being a dog-owner, and he found himself returning the waves and smiles of other pet owners out on nocturnal rambles around the quiet neighborhood. At the small park nearby, he soon recognized familiar faces, enjoying casual conversations while their animals engaged in their own forms of meet and greet.

So far, no complaints from the Body Corporate had been delivered. Teddy was never left alone, and had no reason to fret. How he would behave once Natalie resumed work remained to be seen. Philip sensed that she was ready. Her last check-up was due, and she intended to ask for a clearance to drive.

Philip tried to convince himself he had no reason now to still feel unsettled. He had no major surgical cases booked. His shock over the inheritance had dulled. As soon as possible, he intended to get rid of the cottage and forget the whole episode. His father was dead. How was that fact any different from what he'd believed all his life? Whatever Len McLeod had meant by his gesture — a deathbed regret for deserting his child or a whimsical claim to family — he was gone. All Philip wanted was to get his life back on track with Natalie and perhaps see where they were headed as a couple. Logically, he should be at peace.

Yet the awful dreams bothered him. In the form of anxious images, a presence stalked him, telling him he was going to lose everything he cared for. Sometimes he woke in a sweat, breathing heavily. His subconscious mind concocted stories of pain and loss, where Natalie was fatally injured in a car crash, or she told him she was leaving him for Josh. How could he explain such fears to her?

Even Teddy, who had secretly inserted himself into their bedroom, wore a similar expression when Philip woke again one night. Natalie reached over and stroked Philip's damp hair. 'Another nightmare? You were thrashing around and muttering. What's wrong?'

'I don't know.' He honestly didn't. Caring for Natalie had kept his mind off his own issues. Now that she'd recovered, he felt all the resentments of his past swell up again, pressing for release. Was he going crazy?

When he woke another night, his heart pounding and his chest tight and painful, he wondered if he was having a heart attack. Cautiously he sat up and took several deep breaths. His throat was constricted, as though he was going to be sick. What had he been dreaming about? All he recalled was an escalating sense of danger. Fleeting images lingered on the edge of his consciousness. His father, relentless, pursuing him, insisting Philip stop. Teddy, running crazily through traffic. Natalie in a coffin, white and still. Something terrible, overwhelming, waiting just ahead . . .

He made a swift dash to the bathroom, just in time as his stomach heaved up the remains of dinner. He rinsed his mouth, staring at the gaunt reflection of his face in the yellow strip lighting. Unshaven, his hair on end, he looked awful. His eyes were bloodshot. All the unmanageable emotions he'd buried since childhood came pouring out, assaulting his body with blasts of terror, rage and sorrow. It was far too much to process all at once. He huddled down like a lost child, his head low, his arms clasping his knees, while tears ran freely from his eyes. He knew he would always be like this — completely alone.

He heard the clicking of claws on the tiled floor. Teddy set to work his pink tongue, thoroughly licking Philip's hand. Then he lay down, content to wait there until his master finally stood up, swallowed a glass of water and made his way back to bed. When Teddy vaulted onto the bed and settled his hard little rump against the back of the man who had rescued him, Philip did nothing to discourage the curiously comforting warmth.

He came to a decision as he lay awake, staring into the darkness. In the morning he would go to the hospital and fill out an application for the Ebola training course. He needed a complete break from work, from Natalie, from the past that was hounding him and ruining his chance of happiness. Rumor at the hospital was that places at the

265

Ebola conference were still open. He'd heard differing reasons for the reluctance to go. Family and work commitments were usually cited, but he sensed an underlying fear of the deadly condition, whose death rate in west Africa was quoted at fifty percent. In his opinion, all the more reason for thorough training and preparation.

The decision to offer his services made Philip feel better. What were his puny problems compared to a massive epidemic like this? Natalie could easily spare him for a few days. With a direction in mind, he closed his eyes and fell asleep.

* * *

Philip's step was light as he arrived home from work next day. Teddy barked a welcome while Natalie greeted him with a kiss. 'Had a good day?'

He nodded, signaling to the couch. 'Come and sit down. I want to discuss something.'

She sensed his repressed excitement. Had he received some accolade at work?

'I have an extraordinary opportunity,' he said. 'It's to do with Ebola. The Health Department has a plan to follow United Nations preventive health guidelines. Australia is holding a conference. You could call it a practice run to contain the spread of the disease and protect anyone working with infected patients. I'd like to attend.'

His green eyes were shining with enthusiasm, while Natalie wondered where this left-field topic had come from. Surely, Philip was a surgeon? 'Ebola?' She racked her brains for a context for the strange word. During her convalescence she'd heard of the disease and its fatal impact on communities in west Africa. Like so much of the news, it had been one of the many global tragedies without much personal impact for her. 'What's it got to do with us?' Seeing Philip's expression, she felt guilty. However, he spoke patiently.

'You've missed most of the news reports, Natalie. With international travel, everywhere is at risk. Even here we've had a couple of suspect cases. We need rigorous procedures in place.'

She hesitated. If this was such a dangerous disease, why did he want to place himself at risk? 'I don't understand. You're a surgeon.'

'First and foremost, I'm a doctor,' he corrected her gently. 'Before I specialized, well before we met, I worked for years in the Pacific overseas, in tropical medicine. Nobody else local is free to go, or wants to run the risk.'

'What risk?' Now her memory was sifting through news clips of barren land, impoverished villages, makeshift hospitals. Gruesome reports showed people dead or dying in the streets. Her body was a knot of tension and she clutched his arm.

His tone was calming. 'Let me explain. If, and only if, Ebola emerges in this part of the world, it's critical we know how to treat it without the disastrous results of cross-infection. Australia is training a medical assistance team. Sure, we're well away from the affected areas. But if an epidemic did reach our shores, hospitals would need special units and isolation wards. The Health Department needs to be up to scratch with the very best methods of treatment and containment.'

This side of Philip was a mystery to Natalie. She had to remind herself he worked with top-level decision-makers. Her own needs seemed trivial in comparison. Her recovery was still so recent. How had she become so dependent on him? 'Where is this conference being held?' she asked him.

'In Darwin. We'd be shown the isolation techniques, and there'd be sessions on resources and budgets. Face-to-face exchange means a lot more than theoretical guidelines.'

'Darwin?' The top end of the country, thousands of kilometers north. But it was obvious the call to help had invigorated him. This side of Philip reached out to humanity, and she realized those at home had to step back and let him go. He lived by his belief that his work was a vocation, putting the needs of others before his own. He was a good man, and she felt her heart swell with love for him. 'You really want this, don't you?'

He nodded. 'Yes, I do. My life's been such a mess. I think this will help me get my focus back to what's important.'

'How long would you be away?'

'Less than a week.'

'And you're really the only one who wants to go?'

'The only doctor. Two nurses have registered interest. Patients have to be nursed with no physical contact. Doctors and nurses are suited up in protective gear, even goggles, boots . . . It's like a scene from a science-fiction movie. Of course, our training would only be theoretical.'

'Sounds scary.' She was remembering her own recent hospital experience. Even theater had been a frightening place, with masked and gloved figures looming over her. 'But I still don't see why you would be needed.'

'A hospital needs doctors as well as nurses. It just feels right to be prepared.'

She could hear the passion behind his words. His absence would be a challenge to her, to take her life back instead of hiding in this luxurious retreat. And Philip would be bitterly disappointed if she stopped him from going. She thought of all the recent issues he'd been faced with — stress over the twins, the peculiar facts surrounding his father's life and his mother's secrecy, her own illness. He'd even relented over Teddy. He'd stood by her, carried on, doing what had to be done, but now it was so very evident that he longed for a break and a complete change. And she was on the mend. 'It's settled then,' she said.

'And you'll be fine?'

Natalie smiled, slipping onto his lap and linking her arms around his neck. 'Yes, Philip. I'll be fine.'

He thanked her by putting his arms around her and pulling her close. She leaned into him, absorbing the strength of his warm embrace. Losing him, even if only for a week, was going to be hard, but it was time to set aside her childlike wants. Disentangling herself, she decided to be practical. 'When are you going?'

'I need to be in Darwin by Friday.'

'Then we'd better get organized.' She smiled at him and slipped off his knee. Her mind was listing the issues she'd have to deal with on her own — food supplies, exercise for Teddy, an inspection of the cottage. She'd have to travel by cab, or maybe Josh would help. The list was long, but of course she'd manage. It was time their relationship shifted to a healthier level. She had to chase away this panicky urge to beg him not to leave her.

10

Philip said he would leave early next morning to confirm his decision and re-arrange his hospital commitments. The spring was back in his step. He settled to read the latest reports on the killer disease that had already wiped out several thousand victims in the west African zone, and came to bed late, still radiating energy as he slipped quietly in beside Natalie.

She would have turned to him, but he was obviously preoccupied with the night's events. With a touch of regret, she understood how typical this act was of him — wanting to play a part in stopping such terrible human suffering.

It was barely daybreak when she woke to the beeping of his alarm. She sensed him ease out of bed and, in his considerate way, dress quietly. Ignoring her own impulse to turn over and doze, she pulled on her satin negligee, smoothed her short hair and followed him down to the breakfast table. He seemed surprised to see her.

'You didn't have to get up so early on my account.' He pressed a gentle kiss on her cheek.

'Thought I'd join you for coffee before you go. I guess you have a lot to arrange.'

'I do. I'll settle things at the hospital and pack tonight. The conference starts on Friday evening.'

'Have you ever been to Darwin?' She knew it was in the latitudes that brought tropical storms and torrential rains during the wet season. Even after forty years, Cyclone Tracy was still notorious for devastating the entire city, wiping out its visible history and requiring mass evacuation and rebuilding.

'Never. All I know is it's a six-hour flight across three states, and I expect I'm going to sweat a lot!' He took her in his arms and held her close. 'You haven't reconsidered?'

'I'll be fine. I'm pleased for you.' She pressed against him, wanting him to know he would be missed.

'I'd understand if you needed me to stay.'

Natalie had a flashback to the last time the needs of his work had separated them. Philip had cancelled the Sydney trip and, let's face it, she'd behaved like a spoiled brat then, punishing him by putting out signals to any available male that she was available. The memory made her uncomfortable. Life was forcing her to grow up. And Philip was taking extra care to make sure she was happy with his decision. Perhaps all the struggles of the recent months might have an upside for their relationship.

'It's time I stopped being a couch potato,' she said. 'I've got a cottage to decorate.'

'But you haven't been cleared yet to drive.'

'Then I'll catch cabs, or Josh will give me a lift.'

Philip released her and stepped back. 'Josh? Have you been talking to him?' His tone was casual, but she sensed the underlying concern.

'Yes. We're friends. That's all.'

'Oh.'

She walked with him to the door. He paused, then gave her another kiss — a long one this time. The apartment seemed empty once he'd gone. Reminding herself she had plenty to do, Natalie went upstairs to dress. She needed to get her own life back on track now. Instead of the aimless hours she'd become used to during her convalescence, she had a list of tasks to work through. Teddy needed a walk, she had to prepare a shopping list, and she planned to take up Josh's offer of transport and see the final results of the cottage renovation. Of course the week would pass in a flash.

Collecting the dog's lead, she headed out into a clear spring day. Teddy was in his usual trance state, as though this was the first time his paws had landed on planet Earth. He scuttled from scent to scent, reading who knew what information they contained. She had to wonder at how quickly he'd made the transition to his new home. What was the use of regrets? Was it only humans who clung to the past, reliving unhappy memories that polluted every day?

In retrospect, her dread of hospitals and illness seemed a waste of energy. Not that she aspired to join the medical fraternity! That was an aspect of Philip she couldn't share. He'd said a nurse from his hospital would also attend the Ebola conference. Probably they'd fly up together, maybe share the same living quarters. For a moment Natalie felt excluded, imagining how intensely the delegates would interact.

But this wasn't a morning to indulge in envious thoughts. A feeling of lightness ran through her body as she breathed deeply, soaking up the clarity of colors, trees and gardens. How lucky she was! She ought to focus on the gifts she'd always taken completely for granted

— health, freedom, choices. She knew she trusted Philip. She'd faced and overcome her fears, and the surgery was just a memory. Even the breeze ruffling her cropped hair felt liberating.

She walked as far as the park, where other dogs romped and raced off-lead. She remembered hearing Philip's drama when the dog had almost drowned, and let the lead out to its full length but kept firm hold of the handle. For an hour she let him play until he'd finally had enough and flopped down panting on the grass.

Frequently she thought of Philip, wondering which state he was crossing as the hours passed. It was nearing dinnertime when he phoned her briefly from the Darwin airport, where he had a rushed conversation, competing with the drone of flight announcements and travel chatter. He said the simulated tent hospital was set up in a remote area beyond the city, presumably to enforce the sense of isolation that Ebola inflicted on victims and medical staff alike.

Natalie had barely spoken a few words

when she heard some woman's voice urging him to hurry. 'Sorry, sweetheart. Jane is reminding me the bus is about to leave.' Abruptly he was gone.

It was going to be a long, lonely week. The apartment echoed with Philip's absence. How subtly you became used to living with another person! Natalie pushed away a hollow sense of waiting. A silent television, no dishes in the sink, the bed undisturbed . . . Teddy sensed his new master's absence and mooched on Philip's chair, his head drooping on his paws.

Natalie knew she would welcome a change of scene. A memory of the dog bounding along the sandy shore of the lake with Josh made her dial the painter's number. He'd said something about a surprise. Perhaps he'd offer her a lift, and she could take the dog with her. He was his usual friendly self when he answered, but said he was working with his father on another job. He promised to call her as soon as he was free, and she felt absurdly rejected as she clicked off the phone. She'd been out of contact for months!

Casting around for ways to pass the time, Natalie thought of Irene. This was the ideal opportunity to extend an invitation to her. Would Philip mind? Perhaps he wanted to keep his home life private. He might not like his mother visiting. Natalie was pensive, thinking about the complex man she was falling in love with. Their lives were deeply intertwined. She simply could not imagine being apart from him. Even a week of separation felt like an emptiness only he could fill. She'd never understood, before, why people chose to exchange their carefree court-ship days for long-term commitment. Her independence had felt so impor-tant. Marriage had seemed like the end of fun and the start of duty, babies and bills. But now she knew she was ready for that step.

Was Philip, though? Yes, he'd been kind; he'd looked after her, and called her 'sweetheart'. But did he love her? She sighed. It was the wrong time to hope for an answer to that question. His guard was breaking down. Although his calm, rational front had driven her crazy at times, now she felt she was staring into the heart of a volcano that was about to erupt. His nightmares showed how volatile he really was, and this impulsive decision to rush off to the Ebola conference seemed like an escape from reality. However, whatever happened up in Darwin, whatever he learned, he would have to come home.

Meanwhile, she would extend an invitation to his mother. Perhaps the older woman could offer some advice. A neutral meeting place would be best. She phoned Irene, who sounded delighted to hear from her. They arranged to meet for morning tea at the shopping mall.

*　　*　　*

Natalie woke to another invigorating spring day. A soft breeze ruffled the curtain, and hints of sunlight striped the heavy chocolate-colored quilt. She must have kicked it away some time during the night. It was definitely a man's choice, and the change of season was the perfect excuse to get rid of it. Perhaps she and Philip could buy a lightweight throw in a softer hue. Their trips to the mall were usually practical outings to pick up groceries, and she wondered how he'd take to the suggestion of browsing or window-shopping.

She was sure he would laugh at the concept of retail therapy. Apart from agreeing on the basic style of the furniture for the apartment, they'd made very few domestic decisions together, making do with whatever possessions belonged to their previous lifestyles. Thinking over the past months they'd spent as a couple, Natalie realized life had been a succession of serious issues — the surgical dramas, the death of Philip's father, her own health crisis. Even now, Philip was away on a new mission. How could their personal feelings compare with the Ebola crisis? Was she being selfish, wishing they could spend time together doing simple things? Maybe when Philip came home she could share her thoughts.

She lay half-awake, dreamily absorbing the sounds of birdcalls and traffic drifting up from the street below. How good it felt to nestle in the warmth, knowing she could indulge in a short lie-in while she planned out her day. Life held interest for her again, and her body was gradually getting back to a normal routine. The drugged sensation of her convalescence had gone, and she was enjoying her daily exercise with Teddy. Philip had certainly conceded a great deal by allowing Natalie to care for the dog, who had quickly settled in.

Come to think of it, where was the little fellow? He'd very quickly sussed out the sunny spots where he could stretch out, just as he'd made it known that he preferred canned dog food rather than dry biscuits. He hardly ever barked, saving his excited yaps for the park, where he joined in games with other pets.

Natalie smiled, observing the buried

lump beneath the quilt. He must have burrowed his way there some time during the night. The heap gently rose and fell as he snored softly.

She should get up. Philip was far away, no doubt already immersed in the simulation exercises at the training camp. How well did he know the volunteer nurse from his hospital? If Natalie phoned him, would it seem she was checking up on him? He'd hinted that the course would be intensive. He might not like social calls. Better to leave their timing to him.

She had an appointment with Irene, and Teddy would want to be taken down to the grass as soon as he woke. Enough of lying in bed — she had things to do. Dressing in jeans and a casual striped top, she tidied her short regrowth of hair. In fact she'd come to terms with her new look, especially since Philip had told her he liked it. Pressing teasing kisses on her neck, he'd said it flattered her facial structure and showed off her neat, well-shaped ears. And it was so much easier than using gadgets that added or removed styling waves to longer hair.

She pulled on running shoes, found Teddy's lead and summoned him from sleep, laughing as he peered up at her like a grumpy teenager. 'Walk?'

Hearing the inviting word, he sprang to attention and raced down the stairs full-pelt. She'd only intended a short pit stop, but the crisp morning air enticed her to stride out to the park. Energy flooded her. Perhaps euphoria was a natural swing after her long weeks of sluggish recovery. Before her surgery, she'd had so many definite expectations about life. Now she thought about how little she really needed. A healthy body, food and shelter, and a happy heart more or less covered her list.

Teddy seemed to agree as he explored, at last flopping down at Natalie's feet with body language that said, 'Take me home.' She hoped he would behave while she was out. It would be the first time he'd been left alone in the apartment.

Before she set off to catch the bus to the shopping center, she fed him a liver-flavored chew bar that ought to keep him occupied for a while.

She was looking forward to the outing. One of her fantasies had been meeting her mother at some trendy coffee bar for the daughterly chats she imagined most young women enjoyed. But although they'd re-established contact on better terms, the fact was that Mrs. Norris still lived a thousand kilometers north in Brisbane, and was as committed as ever to her stream of rescued animals. Phone calls were welcome, but coffee mornings with her weren't going to happen.

Irene might be a substitute. Natalie had found her to be open and sympathetic — not a bit like the bitter, closed-off depressive Philip's memory clung to. Apart from the affinity she'd felt for Irene, the meeting would be a roundabout contact with Philip, and might help her understand his present state of mind.

As Natalie entered the Rosella café, the seductive aroma of freshly brewed coffee enveloped her. She paused at the display cabinet, eyeing its array of luscious tarts, flans and elaborate cream cakes. Forget diets! Her old pattern of perfection was gone. She would celebrate the day and enjoy life on her first official return to normal routines.

She found a spare table near the back of the café and watched the doorway. She hardly knew Irene, and wasn't even sure why she'd suggested this meeting. Philip certainly wouldn't approve. But Philip wasn't here, and Irene might offer clues to her son's present state of mind.

A shabby figure was peering tentatively into the café. She waved and made her way toward Natalie. 'Am I late? I mistook the bus stop and had a distance to walk. I don't come into the mall often.' She smoothed down her brown skirt and edged into the bench seat. 'It was kind of you to invite me.'

'I've been housebound since the surgery. It's a relief to get outside.'

'Ah yes. How did that go? Was your operation successful? I remember you were very anxious.'

It felt nice to receive genuine interest. 'Yes. It was rough at first, but I'm recovered now. Philip looked after me very well.'

'I'm glad, my dear. Health is everything.' Her words were heartfelt, and Natalie remembered she had a history of depression.

'I realize that now.'

'Yes. We must count our blessings every day.' Irene hesitated. 'But you felt we should meet to . . . '

Straight to the point! Natalie deflected the query. 'I thought it would be nice to get to know you.'

Irene persisted, 'Are you and my son planning a life together?'

'I'm not sure.'

'It's wise to be cautious. Philip's a good boy, but a life is a long time.' Irene picked up the menu. 'And people change.' She scanned the folder. 'I feel extravagant today. I will have the walnut torte. And you?'

'I think a fruit flan. I'll go and place the order.'

What would Philip say if he saw them sharing cake and confidences? He'd painted an unflattering picture of his mother, and Natalie had her own questions to ask, while Irene had launched straight into the heart of their connection, clearly wanting to know what sort of partner her son was living with. When the coffee arrived, Irene tipped three paper twists of sugar into her black coffee, stirred the liquid and faced Natalie with an intent stare.

'You are a pretty girl,' she decided. 'You have an artistic aura.'

That sounded like a compliment. Natalie wondered how to reply. 'Thank you.'

'I was a model, you know. Not for fashion. Unclothed!' She laughed. 'Men came running, wanting to draw me.

Now look at me. I'm alone. I don't need anything. My son is my only attachment.'

Where was this leading? Was she about to warn Natalie off? If so, this meeting would conclude swiftly. 'I suppose all mothers feel that closeness,' Natalie said, adding, 'to their sons.' Her own mother didn't seem to be at all doting.

Irene was still examining her, the cake on her plate untouched. 'I made many sacrifices to ensure he had a good education. And now he's a surgeon.'

'Yes. You must be proud of him.'

'Philip is doing what he wants. But he offers me money. He doesn't understand . . . ' She reached across the table, resting her thin hand on Natalie's. 'A mother doesn't want money, she wants love.'

This was becoming awkward. She could hardly sit Philip down and order him to love his mother. He didn't like visiting Irene, and he wasn't demonstrative with his feelings. Perhaps Natalie could swing the conversation around to her own point of view. 'Philip doesn't talk about love. I find he shows it in what he does.' She was remembering all the considerate caring he'd shown her, and suddenly her speech dried up as she understood — Philip must love her. He must love her deeply. Why else would he have cared for her so devotedly, while she'd moaned and complained and hardly said a word of thanks?

She'd always judged a man's affection by his sexual interest in her. As soon as personal issues cropped up, the relationship had simply died, and she'd moved on to the next admirer. But surely Philip was different. Yes, she could turn him on easily enough. But when that changed, when she wasn't well, he'd cared about her. She wanted him back, at home. He needed to see that she cared about him, too.

Irene was following Natalie's distracted silence, her expression curious. 'You mean, when he offers me money, he's really offering me love?'

'In a way. He seems to be . . . unresolved about his father. And why you kept that secret.' There! It was out in the open.

Irene nodded. 'I thought so. But he says nothing. I see now I was wrong. I thought I was protecting him.'

'From his father?'

'From the law. From the views of other people. It's hard for you to understand.'

'Philip knows his father was . . . ' What was the term Irene would use? 'Gay' hardly described the pain of Len's life, or Irene's, or Philip's.

'Deviant. Queer.' Irene's voice was sad. 'Those were the words people used back then. The words I used, to my shame. I felt deceived.'

'And Philip felt abandoned.' Irene's attitudes might have softened, but she needed to understand why her son was angry.

Irene forked a piece of her torte into her mouth and chewed slowly. 'He's confided in you, then. All I've had is chats and offers of money.'

Natalie had a flash of insight. 'Why

not accept them? Surely that would be a starting point?' She knew Philip didn't want his father's gift. But to him, helping his mother financially would prove his gratitude for the sacrifices she had made. And in a roundabout way, Len would have paid his dues.

'You see, Natalie, I want for nothing really. I have a roof over my head and my budgie for company. I have friends at the housing estate.'

'Perhaps you could travel?'

Irene was thoughtful. 'Yes. Perhaps. I do think of my homeland with nostalgia.'

The background chatter in the café had built up, and it seemed easier to eat and drink in silence. Enough had been said. Irene had built a life that suited her, in the same way that Natalie's mother found fulfillment in her animals. Natalie's thoughts drifted to Teddy. How was he behaving?

'You're smiling,' commented Irene.

'I was just thinking of our dog. He's home alone. I hope he's not tearing the place to shreds.'

'Philip has a dog? Will wonders never cease!' Irene picked up the few remaining crumbs on her plate and wiped her mouth with a paper napkin. Gathering her shabby carrier bag, she stood up. 'I've enjoyed meeting you again, Natalie.'

As Natalie prepared to follow her, a small child at a nearby table knocked over a milkshake and burst into tears as the mother scolded her. Natalie sighed. Being a parent seemed awfully difficult. She remembered Philip asking her if she was pregnant. What if her answer had been yes? Could she ever be a mother? Could they be parents? She'd come through one of the hardest times in her life, thanks to Philip. He'd been there to lean on; to encourage her; to care in all the small, unobtrusive ways that said he loved her. Was that when she'd fallen in love with him? Thinking of him, so far away, caused an ache in her heart. She missed him more than she'd ever believed she could. The future was suddenly full of possibilities.

11

When Philip checked in at the conference center, he was sent to a barracks-like tent lined with camp beds. The rudimentary bathroom offered cold-water sinks, and the lavatories were pit-style. Obviously the intention was to create the kinds of makeshift conditions likely to be experienced in an overseas epidemic.

Lying awake that night, pestered by mosquitoes and the snores of several delegates, he felt a sense of novelty and adventure. He'd been right to come. A few short hours in a plane, and he was in a make-believe world, about to confront a deadly scourge. He knew nobody here. Jane, the nurse he'd travelled with, was in separate sleeping quarters on the far side of the grounds. He could just as well be on that huge, tropical moon ascending the royal-blue evening sky. At the latrine, lizards hung motionless on the walls, like Aboriginal rock art. Unfamiliar birds called from the darkening silhouettes of branches. *Watch out for snakes*, a colleague had warned, noting his thongs. This was definitely a different environment.

How petty his troubles were, compared to the real problems of the world. His work as a doctor had this great blessing of lifting him out of himself. From this vantage point, he could hardly remember why he'd been feeling so upset. He could think of his father's legacy in a detached way. Here his mother was a faded figure, deserving his gratitude rather than criticism. Natalie had tried to make him see that. Well, he would tell her she was right. He was wasting his life in recriminations. Natalie wasn't far off the mark when she accused him of sulking.

She was changing before his eyes. He'd seen the huge effort she'd made since her surgery. She'd overcome her phobia and won through a difficult convalescence. She had always brought color and laughter and beauty to his life. Until a few months ago, he'd thought of her as lovely but immature. He'd certainly not entertained any long-term plans with her. But their crisis had changed all that. Caring for her had made Philip access his loving side. Somehow they'd become a small family, complete with dog. Could he go back to his solitary ways, living for his job, filling in his evenings with reading research articles and watching television?

Hoping he would be spared the nightmares that had been plaguing him, Philip dozed fitfully, with no unpleasant dreams. He woke early to a day that warned him not to venture far without sunscreen and a hat, as long as the sun shone. The clouds would no doubt roll in and dump their daily downpour on the town — probably a thunderstorm, as was usual in the tropics. Even before breakfast the humidity was climbing.

He found the canteen and served himself a simple breakfast, then moved on to the conference tent. There he was handed his parcel of isolation gear.

Inevitably, a patient suspected of carrying the deadly Ebola virus posed a threat to every contact. To enforce the simulation, health workers were told to don their heavy overalls, goggles, headgear, gloves and boots. Within minutes, Philip began to sweat. As he tried to focus on the hour-long address by a contagious disease expert, he began to feel faint. He reminded himself these were the conditions endured by those working overseas in the heart of the epidemic. Ebola was transmitted through body fluids, and the health workers were warned of the extreme danger of any contact. They had to maintain strict isolation techniques, adding a psychological burden to the nauseating physical symptoms.

Philip felt completely isolated in his discomfort. How his fellow health workers were faring was anybody's guess. He thought he recognized Jane, but it was hard to distinguish anybody as they shuffled in their clumsy boots, their eyes obscured by goggles. The body language he took for granted was erased by the

298

heavy protective gear encasing every-one. His breathing was thick and clammy, and his peripheral vision was restricted. A surgical mask blocked his sense of smell. Even sound was muffled. He'd attempted to take down notes, his gloved fingers fumbling to guide the pen. Working in an operating theatre would be unthinkable under these conditions.

The next session would involve setting up an emergency hospital tent and equipment. Working in their protective gear, the nurses in the group were sent to work through admission assessments, set up transfusions, and provide palliative nursing care to their patients, represented by several manikins designed for use in resuscitation lectures.

With other doctors, Philip attended a separate workshop on treatments and drug regimes, dosages and side effects. From there, they were directed to join the nurses and submit to full-body sponges, again to reinforce the strange sense of isolation engendered by the clumsy gear. Under normal circumstances that exercise would have raised plenty of laughs. As it was, the nurses worked mechanically, and Philip guessed they were hot, perspiring, and as eager as he'd been to disrobe from their bulky gear.

He'd expected medical and administrative lectures, but was surprised by the extent of psychological emphasis in the program. The isolating effects of Ebola, felt by ill patients, were also suffered by staff. The day-in, day-out confinement, coupled with uncomfortable conditions and fear of infection, took a high toll on volunteers, despite their best intentions. The delegates had little opportunity to socialize. It wasn't easy to chat when you were struggling to put on the cumbersome hoods, aprons and protective suiting which, as Jane quipped, made her feel like a chicken in a roasting bag. Mobile phones were off-limits except for family emergencies. In any case, without recharge facilities, cell phones weren't much use.

As a doctor, Philip focused on the

diagnosis of conditions likely to accompany a full-blown case of Ebola. Case histories told grim stories. Recovery almost seemed to be a matter of luck. Some struggled back to health, but a great many more were ravaged by dysentery, malnutrition, dehydration, and the sudden hemorrhage that carried off the vulnerable. Daily showings of film clips, interviews and videos reinforced the horror of the worst-hit regions, where the dead were piled up in the streets. He hoped with all his heart that the epidemic could be contained. Ebola scythed through whole populations, ravaging families and leaving bewildered orphans in its wake.

The conference ended on a somber note, and Philip was pleased when Jane invited him to join her on a scenic walk at a nearby nature reserve. His flight was booked for the weekend, and he hadn't seen much of Darwin — just a brief bus tour of significant stopping points with little time to explore. Howard Springs Nature Reserve was less than an hour's run south of the city. Philip and Jane shared a taxi out to the site, deciding to go together when Jane's friend dropped out. The driver dropped them at a pleasant picnic area near a shop and restaurant. 'Watch your step on the trails,' he warned. 'Rain will have made them slippery.' The weather was on the cusp of the wet season, and signs warned hikers to keep to the marked paths.

After the stress of the past days, this place was like a little piece of heaven. Tame sacred ibis stalked the parking area, and the bush was melodious with whistling and caroling birds. A sign pointed the way to a loop trail and a spring-fed swimming pool.

'I brought my bathers.' Jane grinned as she unearthed a bikini from her duffle bag. 'How about you?'

'I've got a rain jacket, insect spray and my cell phone.'

Jane laughed at him. 'You must have been a Boy Scout.'

'No, but I like to be prepared.'

'It's only a little stroll in the bush.'

She was teasing him, her mood as light as his own. They'd both made it through the challenging course and would take essential information back to the hospital. And tomorrow Philip would step off the plane into Natalie's waiting arms. The nightmares that had plagued him for weeks had stopped. Perhaps the daily exposure to the reality of Ebola had relieved his mind of the need to dream up imaginary horrors. His cares seemed remote and trivial.

He indicated the shop. 'Would you like coffee and something to eat before we head off? My treat.'

'Why not? Gooey cake, I hope.' She wiggled her plump hips and giggled. 'I'll forget my diet today.'

In the shop they ordered coffee and slices of an extravagantly rich gâteau. Jane chose a table by the windows. Beyond the car park, woodlands formed a gentle screen for the dense rainforest stretching away into the distance. 'What made you sign up for this conference?' Philip asked her. From time to time they'd worked side by side in the intensive care ward. Apart from noting she was capable and efficient, he'd never given her a second thought. He rarely speculated on other people's lives. Now, after the experience they'd shared, he wondered about other aspects of her nature.

'My husband's an ambulance driver. We both share a similar philosophy. Oh, that sounds pretentious.'

'Not at all. How would you describe it — your philosophy?'

Jane hesitated. 'There's a saying: to move a mountain, start by carrying away small stones. Something like that. Matt and I feel so privileged, living in Australia. We can't do much for the world, but at least we can pick up on opportunities to help, if they cross our paths.'

They sounded like decent people. It was time for Philip to step down from his ivory tower. He felt more connected, somehow.

Jane moved her hand, indicating his mouth. 'A blob of cream, Doctor.' She laughed as he wiped it away and went to pay at the counter. Like the taxi driver, the man at the counter recommended they stay on the walking trails, and added further advice. 'I'd head back by lunchtime. You can get doused quickly if the rain comes.'

'Are you expecting rain?' Philip asked. The sky was without a single cloud.

'Some days it's heavy. The Wet's just started. Next month we close most of the trails.'

'Then we'll get going.'

Jane had joined him. 'I'll buy a bottle of water,' she said. 'Want one?'

The shop owner agreed. 'Always wise to carry water.'

Philip was reminded how little he knew about bushwalking, or any physical hobby. It was high time he developed some leisure interests. Natalie might have some ideas. He rather fancied strolling with her and Teddy through leafy glades. They might take a basket of food, as they did in movies, and enjoy a romantic picnic by a stream.

As time passed, however, he was less sure. The loop trail was trickier than he'd expected. As he'd been warned, the ground underfoot was moist and slippery. Clumps of leaves slid away under his shoes, and he had to take care not to lose his balance. Jane was wearing rubber-soled joggers, but his own shoes had leather soles and lacked any grip. He found himself clinging to boulders and overhead branches as he negotiated areas where the ground sloped. Jane took the obstacles in her stride and kept stopping to wait for him. She seemed to find the going quite easy. He wished they could turn back, but she was evidently enjoying the challenge.

'You go bushwalking regularly?' Philip asked her.

'It's one of our hobbies. Matt has to keep fit for his job, and I like getting out in the fresh air.'

'We should keep an eye on the time.' Philip was imagining a downpour adding to his discomfort.

Jane just laughed. 'Heaps of time before any rain comes! There's the arrow pointing to the springs. I'm going to have a dip.'

Philip saw a new track veering at right angles to the main path. 'It doesn't say how far they are. Perhaps we should leave it, Jane.'

'It can't be far. Surely you're not tired?'

'Of course not.' Doggedly he followed her. Using boulders as stepping-stones, she easily negotiated the puddles that filled depressions in the path and plunged ahead, under the canopy of tall trees. Ghost gums and other eucalypts soared up, seeming to block the sunlight. Philip tramped on, his leather soles slipping and sliding. A tangle of vines lassoed his ankle, and an ungainly stick-like insect was teetering on his arm. With dislike, he flicked it away.

Jane noticed. 'They're so cute! I love the way they merge with their environment.'

She sounded fond of the creature.

Did people really do this sort of thing for pleasure? Philip would have to think of an alternative exercise to suggest to Natalie. She wouldn't enjoy this at all.

The track suddenly veered downhill, bypassing immense rocky outcrops. Philip edged his way forward, crouching and clinging to any handhold he could find. He dearly hoped there would be an alternative route back to the main entrance. If going downhill was difficult, what would the return journey be like?

'I can see the pool!' Jane sounded elated as she called back to him. 'Do you need a hand to climb down here?'

'I'm doing fine,' Philip assured her. He steadied his left foot against a tree root, took a step and felt his right foot slide away on an unstable pile of wet leaves. Collapsing on the ground, he felt an agonizing pain shoot through his ankle. All he could do was rock back and forth, grimacing and panting, and hoping that he could find some way back to civilization and medical help.

Jane hurried back to examine the injury. She barely touched the ankle, yet his yells of pain made her draw back with a sigh of worry. 'It could be a break, but I'm more inclined to think it's severely sprained,' she said. 'Either way, you can't walk on it, Philip.'

'What am I supposed to do? Fly? I can't sit here in the bush forever.'

'Of course not. You'll have to be carried or winched out.'

'Great! What do we do? Send smoke signals?'

'It could be worse, Philip. It's not like we're stranded in a national park. We're only a few kilometers from help. We need to get you comfortable, then I'll dash back and get help.'

Her manner was soothing, but he knew she was glossing over the difficulties. The odds of a helicopter being able to land in this rocky area weren't good. It would take more than one man to carry him out; she would need to liaise with the SES or some other trained team. One thing was sure

— it would take time. Philip was in for a long, damp and solitary sojourn in the bush, without medical help or even a support bandage to ease his discomfort.

'I think you should crawl under there.' Jane pointed to the overhanging rock face, patiently ignoring Philip's groan at the thought of moving. 'At least you'll be out of the sun or the rain. Let me check out our bags. I think I've got some painkillers.'

Gratefully he swallowed the tablets while Jane arranged her swimming towel, his jacket and the water bottles. But there was nothing she could do to help as he levered himself over the uneven ground, trying to make light of his obvious pain. 'If this is a healthy outing in the fresh air, you can have it!'

'It's rotten luck.' Concern showing in her expression, Jane watched him settle himself in the makeshift shelter. 'Do you have the number of the reserve on your phone?'

'Yes; I phoned them to make inquiries.'

'Good. Then we can let them know what's happened. They can get right on with organizing the rescue, and I'll go back and show them where you are.'

'Thanks.' But his spirits dived further as he realized he would be alone for hours. He stared suspiciously at the strange conical earth construction a few meters from his feet. 'What's that thing?'

'Just a termite nest.'

'Is that all?' Sarcasm covered Philip's fear. He had no idea what dangers might be hiding here. What if his impromptu shelter also housed a nest of red-bellied snakes or funnel-web spiders?

Jane didn't reassure him when she finished her call and handed his cell phone back to him. 'Don't run the battery flat. Save it for emergencies.'

'This isn't an emergency?'

She was about to leave. He couldn't help asking, 'How long do you think you'll be?'

'Just as quick as I can. Oh — and Philip, watch out for leeches.' With a quick wave, she was gone.

The silence closed in around him. How long would it take Jane to reach help, arrange for a rescue team, and return to where he was stranded? Several hours, he thought. At least he had daylight on his side. He didn't fancy a night alone in the bush. God knew what creepy-crawlies were hiding nearby, just waiting to explore this intruder in their domain.

He thought he heard voices echoing from the direction of the pool and his hopes rose. There might be other walkers nearby. But nobody appeared, and the echoes faded. He remembered he was on a side track, disconnected from the main loop. In any case, it would take more than amateurs to steer him back to safety. The biggest hurdle would be scaling the overhang of rock. They might have to take him forward as far as the swimming pool and use an alternative path to carry him out.

Time dragged. Was it only ten minutes since he'd checked his watch?

His ankle throbbed terribly, and he debated whether to endure the agony of dragging his foot free from the shoe or leaving the injury to swell. It was a bad sprain. Lucky he hadn't snapped the talus. As it was, he'd need crutches and professional strapping.

He hoped he'd manage to catch his plane tomorrow. As his thoughts drifted homewards, Natalie's lovely face formed in his imagination. She'd attracted him from the first minute he'd set eyes on her. All the time they'd discussed furnishings and décor, he'd wanted to stare at her, memorizing her outstanding beauty. Rapid sequences crossed his mind like a film — her expression, lost in lovemaking, and her dark, tragic gaze as he'd left her that day she'd faced up to surgery.

He shifted and moaned. Why had he agreed to this cursed outing? He raked his nails up and down his arms, only making the itching more intense. Some invisible pests had bitten any exposed flesh they could find. Too late, he sprayed himself with repellent. He had a drink of water and eyed his phone. It was much too early for Jane to be calling him with rescue plans. Perhaps he could let Natalie know what was going on. Or would she only worry?

Strange how restless the bush was. Branches cracked, leaves rustled, and flickers and flashes suggested the movement of creatures he could not see. The birds seemed to call and answer one another. One in particular had a single drawn-out tone that ended sharply, like a whip crack. He knew nothing about their species; had never bothered to put names to the city birds that hopped and pecked under the feet of shoppers at the mall.

A nondescript brown bird fluttered down as Philip watched, landing near him. Instinctively, he stayed still while it pecked around the leaf litter. What did birds eat? Worms? Insects? He had no idea. It might be building a nest. Did it have a mate? He was sorry when it flew back to the canopy. At least it had been a kind of company while he waited.

He began to see more signs of life. Lizards, the kind often seen in Aboriginal art, moved with angular, darting twists. He saw a tiny mouse-like creature poke its quivering nose from a fallen log and dash into the untidy undergrowth. He followed the progress of another of those odd stick insects he'd flicked away, earning Jane's disapproval. This one was much bigger — at least twelve centimeters long, with delicate jointed legs on which it rocked and teetered like a clown in the Cirque du Soleil.

A thick drop of water stung his cheek, announcing the arrival of the rain. Just a shower, he hoped. He could still make out patches of blue sky through the canopy. Pulling himself deeper under his shelter, he sat staring at the rock face. He had the impression of a face: a slash of mouth, protuberance of nose, and two round staring eyes, seeming to weep as the water slowly trickled down its surface. What if stones were a form of life? Did the boulders he'd touched sit there, frozen, observing and recording with some primeval consciousness?

The rain was pelting down now, splashing into puddles. A soft hushing sound surrounded Philip as hidden watercourses swelled and flowed downhill. The stick insect was disoriented as it stumbled this way and that, reeling from the blows of heavy raindrops. Philip picked up a long twig. Groaning with pain, he edged out and placed the stick under the creature's front legs. It clung on, its color fading to match the dappled surface it now rode. Philip pulled it in beside him and watched as it mindlessly tried to mount the rock face and fell back. At least it was out of the rain. He pressed himself closer to the rock, giving a yell as his ankle twisted. The pain was making him dizzy.

After a few minutes, the roar of the downpour eased. Weak sunlight was emerging as Philip gazed up through the canopy. The leaves were shimmering and breaking up into a million points of light. Everything was dazzling. Birdcalls merged into a pure harmony, and a sense of belonging filled him. He would be fine. In a few hours the rescuers would come. Tomorrow he would be home with Natalie and the dog. He was starting life over.

Looking back, he saw a lonely, repressed stranger, his feelings locked away. How had he felt so isolated? Here, stranded in the bush, he'd found a friend in Jane, who even now was setting aside her own comfort to face the long walk to bring him help. He could never be abandoned when he was part of these birds, these insects, all the creatures that crawled and hopped. Even this rock that gave him shelter. His work wasn't enough, though the Ebola simulation was a huge catalyst, driving home how millions of people had no choice but to suffer and endure.

Philip could choose. His hurts were trivial things. He'd needed Natalie and his father to remind him of that. He needed people — his accident was proof of that. Suddenly he felt an overpowering need to call Natalie. She did not answer, but he heard her warm voice inviting the caller to record a message. He knew exactly what he wanted to say.

'Philip here. See you tomorrow. I love you, Natalie. Will you marry me?'

He smiled as he clicked off the phone. The irony of his situation struck him. Here he was, holed up in the bush, immobile, and as far away from Natalie as he could be — and he'd had the audacity to actually propose! Most women would be scandalized at the lack of planning and the total absence of romance. Why hadn't he waited until he could set up a special moment? There was supposed to be a sunset, and a ring, and down-on-bended-knee stuff. Even he, prize idiot that he was romantically, knew that. Well, providing Natalie would have him, he would arrange that, as soon as he could. But he simply knew this was right. He was absolutely sure he loved Natalie. He wanted to marry her. She was his joy and his love. About that, he had no doubts at all.

Epilogue: One Year Later

The opening of the Len McLeod Cottage would take place on this fine Sunday afternoon in October. In keeping with the significance of the event for the small lakeside community, nature had kindly provided a mild, sunny day with a breeze to stir the ripples and shadows on the water.

Denise Courtney, who was in the process of packing up and selling her home, was allowing herself to postpone work for the rest of the day. Her decision to move to Melbourne and live near her sister hadn't required much soul-searching. She'd known for a while that a change was coming. Len's death had been an important factor, but not the only one. She was starting to feel her age and would feel happier with family within her orbit. But the packing up was a nuisance. One gathered so much detritus! All the jugs that had never poured milk, and the vases that had never displayed a bunch of flowers! And she had enough spare linen and blankets to accommodate a regiment. It all had to go. Her future life would be a simpler affair, in every sense.

She'd carried a torch for Len too long, though, to miss this public honoring of his talent. As for the private side of his life, it was nobody's business but his, just as the significant part she'd played in his life would never be common knowledge. It was fitting and right, she thought, that Len would have a permanent place where he'd lived much of his life, in this tiny community clustered on the fringes of the gentle lake. The council had moved swiftly for once, when it seemed the word was out that other buyers were on the lookout for desirable properties with water views. They'd paid a decent price, considering the expense that Len's son had gone to, and the work his talented fiancée had contributed.

The engagement of Philip and Natalie had been a heart-warming piece of news. Perhaps she could pass on a few of her treasured items to them. At least love was still alive. They'd walked up to give her the news of their engagement, Teddy in tow. Denise had looked at the pair, the love light shining in their eyes, and she'd seen that sometimes a romance really did work out.

She wouldn't have predicted it, though. At first they'd seemed ill-suited. The changes seemed to have been triggered in both cases by misfortune. Poor Natalie had suffered for months after her surgery. She was better now, and her hair had grown again: she looked beautiful, young and confident. But it was the change in her personality that struck Denise. She was much more frank and assertive with Philip, and she'd firmly reined in her flirtatious ways with Josh.

Denise remembered the way Philip had limped around, disabled, for weeks after his bush injury. She'd offered sympathy, fully expecting his usual rebuff. Instead he'd been quite appreciative, and even told her about his trip north for the Ebola training. He seemed to have lost that abrupt manner that had probably covered a feeling of social inadequacy.

He was as pleased as Denise that his father would have a lasting memorial here at Len McLeod Cottage. Perhaps Len had never been able to lead life on his own terms, or know his son, but his paintings would endure. Sometimes wounds had the power to bestow gifts or heal. She sighed. She would always miss Len, and she would miss living in this tightly knit community whose lake was a non-judgmental mirror to quiet lives that sometimes hid deep desires. It was an atmosphere that had suited Len's later work. His abstracts had deep implications, though she privately preferred his earlier realistic paintings.

A number of the drawings she'd handed over to Philip had been sold for a goodly sum. She'd also heard that a trust fund had been set up for the ongoing maintenance of Len's former home. What would they do with the place? Perhaps fill it with reproductions and historical information. Well, she wouldn't be here to see it.

A car was pulling up, much too early. The ceremony wasn't due to start for a couple of hours. Of course Philip and Natalie would want to make last-minute checks that everything was shipshape. Teddy bounded out of the vehicle with a possessive volley of barks. He was the very image of a contented, well-loved pet. That was a worry off Denise's mind. Natalie had even mentioned they were planning to move to a house with a garden. Yes, life had a way of working out!

Now a third figure emerged from the car. Could it be Philip's mother? He'd said Irene had agreed to attend the opening ceremony of her former husband's memorial gallery. There she was — a small, neat figure walking alone, bearing her own memories. What would she say if she knew the truth of Denise's feelings for Len, and her place in his life? Would she care? At least she was here with her son today.

Denise smiled as she watched Philip and Natalie pause to examine a recent burst of spring color in the garden. Philip pulled her to him protectively, and they shared a lingering kiss. Then Natalie was tugging him by the hand. Philip hadn't been here for a few weeks; he wouldn't have seen the surprise waiting in the backyard. Josh had come last week, carting his brushes and pots of paint, to complete the trompe l'oeil he'd started almost a year ago to surprise Natalie.

Afterwards, Denise had gone to see the finished artwork. She'd stood and stared, thinking she'd wandered into the wrong garden. He had painted this vision of space and beauty on the ugly cement-block wall. Now a vista of trees and birds framed a limpid body of water, forever lapping at a stony shore. Not so different from its model — the timeless waters of the real lake below.

Denise offered her warm praise, and Josh had told her he was going to follow his heart and try his luck in Sydney, doing similar installations. So much change! Comings, goings . . . A phase was closing, and the players were starting afresh.

Now it was time to get dressed up and do her makeup. Love had many faces. However you liked to define her relationship with Len McLeod, Denise loved him. She wasn't going to celebrate his life wearing anything but her best.

We do hope that you have enjoyed reading this large print book.

Did you know that all of our titles are available for purchase?

We publish a wide range of high quality large print books including:
Romances, Mysteries, Classics
General Fiction
Non Fiction and Westerns

Special interest titles available in large print are:
The Little Oxford Dictionary
Music Book, Song Book
Hymn Book, Service Book

Also available from us courtesy of Oxford University Press:
Young Readers' Dictionary
(large print edition)
Young Readers' Thesaurus
(large print edition)

For further information or a free brochure, please contact us at:
Ulverscroft Large Print Books Ltd.,
The Green, Bradgate Road, Anstey,
Leicester, LE7 7FU, England.
Tel: (00 44) **0116 236 4325**
Fax: (00 44) **0116 234 0205**

Other titles in the
Linford Romance Library:

INTRIGUE IN ROME

Phyllis Mallett

Gail Bennett's working holiday in Rome takes an unexpectedly sinister turn as soon as she arrives at her hotel. Why does the receptionist give out her personal details to someone on the phone? Who is the mysterious man she spies checking her car over? Soon she meets Paul, a handsome Englishman keen to romance her — but he is not what he seems. And how does Donato — Italian, charming — fit into the picture? Gail knows that one of them can save her, while the other could be the death of her . . .